OUT O

MERLIN RADICAL FICTION

edited by
John Lucas

Out of Work by John Law (Margaret Harkness) (1888)
Sandwichman by Walter Brierley (1937)
The Story of a Modern Woman
by Ella Hepworth Dixon (1894)
The Wild Goose Chase Rex Warner (1937)

OUT OF WORK

by

JOHN LAW
(Margaret Harkness)

Introduction by
Bernadette Kirwan

LONDON

MERLIN PRESS

Published in 1990
by the Merlin Press Ltd.
10 Malden Road
London NW5 3HR
First published in 1888
by Swan Sonnenschein & Co.
Introduction © 1990 by Bernadette Kirwan
Printed in Denmark by
Nørhaven A/S, Viborg
ISBN 0 85036 389 6

GENERAL INTRODUCTION

The aim of *Merlin Radical Fiction* is soon stated. It is to make available for present-day readers a number of once well-known novels which have been languishing out of print, if not out of mind. Not all novels that were famous in their day deserve or need resurrecting; the ones we have chosen to re-print are important, not merely because they were once celebrated, but because they have qualities that make them durable works of fiction. We certainly do not intend to re-print novels that can be called radical only because of their "message". We understand radicalism in a more rewarding way, one that includes the means of telling as much as what is told. For example, Rex Warner's *The Wild Goose Chase* is a wonderfully inventive political and social allegory, entirely different in conception from the social realism of Walter Brierley's *Sandwichman*. Yet Brierley's method works. It is admirably suited to the grim, moving story he has to tell. Different as they are from each other, Margaret Harkness's (John Law's) *Out of Work* and Ella Hepworth Dixon's *The Story of a Modern Woman* are adroit and compelling works of fiction in their own right.

It is part of our ambition for the series to range as widely as possible, over time, style, authors. Later re-prints will be of fiction of the 1790s, at one extreme, and of the 1950s, at the other. We also hope to include novels from North America and, in translation, novels from Europe. Each book will be introduced by a writer who is an authority on the novel and its author, and the introductions will blend biographical and critical matter.

It is our hope that in the coming years the Radical Fiction Series will enable new generations of readers

"To confer with who are gone.
And the dead living into counsel call."

John Lucas

INTRODUCTION

by

BERNADETTE KIRWAN

In April 1888 Engels wrote to Margaret Harkness—the author of *Out of Work* who wrote under the male pseudonym of John Law*—in reply to her request for a critical appraisal of her first novel, *A City Girl* (1887). Engels praised her effort, but made the specific criticism that it was 'not quite real enough. Realism to my mind, implies truth of detail, the truthful reproduction of typical characters under typical circumstances.'[1] He argued that Harkness's representation of a passive working class was inapplicable to London in 1887, adding that he did not expect to read a 'point-blank socialist novel . . . to glorify the social and political views of the author' and cited Balzac as the exemplary realist novelist, who was better able than Zola to anatomize his society. He concluded his letter with the generous admission:

> I must own in your defence, that nowhere in the civilized world are the working people less actively resistant, more passively submitting to fate, more *hébétés* than in the East End of London. And how do I know whether you have not had very good reasons for contenting yourself, for once, with a picture of the passive side of working class life, reserving the active side for another work?

Out of Work (1888) is in many ways that other work, offering 'a picture, not like *A City Girl* of a social section, but of a social situation, the consequences of unemployment.'[2] Margaret Harkness was well placed to write such a novel since she struggled to earn a living during

---

* The novel is dedicated to John Law of Lauriston, a Scottish economist (1671–1729). Presumably Harkness intends a complex joke.

the eighteen-eighties amongst the East End poor, working as a journalist and living estranged from her family. John Goode[2] and Beate Kaspar[3] have begun to piece together Harkness's life from the scant, available material, which includes Harkness's own journalism and novels, and the diary and letters of her distant cousin, Beatrice Webb. The brief account of her life which follows draws heavily on this pioneering work.

Margaret Harkness was born on 28 February 1854 at Upton-on-Severn in Worcestershire, where her father was a rector. Her parents are described in Webb's diary as 'clerical and conventional'[4] people. She was intellectually stifled by a repressive upbringing, and in order to escape this environment she moved to London sometime during 1877 to train as a nurse at the Westminster Hospital. In 1878 she was confiding her dissatisfaction to Webb about her chosen career: "I own I do not think I have any love of nursing in my constitution, I can do it . . . I feel more interested in watching the minds and manners of the patients than their complaints. . ."

By 1881 Harkness was working as a journalist, writing articles on social questions for the journals *Nineteenth Century* and *National Review*,[5] as well as producing two books for the Religious Tract Society's Bypaths of Bible Knowledge series on Egyptian and Assyrian life. This career change seems to have benefitted her enormously, and in 1883, Beatrice Webb recorded that since Harkness had 'broken loose from all ties, supporting herself by literary piecework . . . she is blossoming out into a clever, interested and amusing woman'. In relation to their shared interest in the plight of the poor in the East End, she wrote: 'she attaches much more importance to individuals, resenting what she has nicknamed "my phantom theory."' From 1887–1889 Harkness published three novels dealing with the lives of the working class poor in the East End.

They are: *A City Girl, Out of Work* and *Captain Lobe: a story of the Salvation Army* (1889). Then, in 1890, she published *A Manchester Shirtmaker*, dealing with the same subject, although on this occasion the setting was Manchester. In between writing these novels, she researched and wrote accounts of the working lives of young men and women in London which were published in *The British Weekly* from 1887 through to 1888. She was active in the Social Democratic Federation (SDF) by this time, working closely with H.H. Champion; and was an active supporter in the 1889 dock strike. But from accounts in Webb's diary, 1889 seems to have been a year of personal troubles and conflicts for Harkness. When Webb visited her in Manchester where she was researching and writing her Manchester novel, Webb recorded:

> Poor Maggie gets bitterer and bitterer with the whole world—does foolish and inconsiderate things and then is vexed when she loses friends. Poor Maggie! with her lonely tortuous life and envious temper. And yet for those in trouble she has plenty of warm sympathy—true *mitgefühl* for the failures of society.

About a month after the date of this diary entry, Harkness was writing a 'Letter to the Editor' of *Justice*, the weekly paper of the SDF, about her dissatisfaction with the organization and its members:

> We are not a happy family and sometimes our quarrels make it difficult for us to "sacrifice without cursing." To find oneself without a relation or a friend, because one is by conviction a Socialist, then to find vials of wrath poured on one's head by Socialists, mak·s one inclined to curse.[6]

Harkness's relationship with her political comrades seems to have been fraught with difficulties, as was the organization of the labour movement at this time. In November 1889 Webb was writing:

The last year she has been hand in glove with the underground labour party, with Champion, Burns, Mann etc., "The only way to observe them is to pretend to be immensely interested, but aren't they suspicious. . ." Poor Maggie! A strange weariness and chronic depression adds pathos to her curious contortions. . .

This record, however, followed Harkness's letter to *The Star* in September, printed under her own name. In it she declared 'I joined the SDF and discovered it to be a dead body in a few months. Then I left it.'[7] Yet by February 1890, Webb's diary entry records:

Margaret Harkness spent two nights here. She is in a much more satisfactory state. Her position with the new trade unionists, and the genuine affection the leaders have for her has softened and enlarged her life, and her faith in their aims has transformed her from a cold-blooded journalist in search of copy to an honourable colleague.

It has not been possible to ascertain how Harkness managed to restore relations with her political allies, but by September 1890 her volatile commitment was once again revealed. She wrote to Webb telling her that she was leaving England permanently, and in the following month an article appeared in the *Pall Mall Gazette*, written under her pseudonym, praising the work of the Salvation Army and promoting its approach to the problems of poverty and unemployment, to the detriment of a socialist solution. This article reads like a renunciation of her socialist past, but it also recalls an earlier article in *Justice* entitled 'Salvationists and Socialists', in which she had written:

The two organizations ought to work more together than they do at present, for they have many points of common interest. For our respect the army teaches us a great lesson. It has never split up. It is one large labour union.[8]

In the 1890 article, 'Salvation vs. Socialism—In Praise of General Booth' she explained that her 'socialist

dream' had gradually diminished after having worked
with the socialist leaders of the dock strike, and
discovered that their political philosophy of co-
operation and united action belied their personal
actions, which were motivated by 'Individualism.' She
argues in favour of the introduction of General Booth's
scheme of coercive labour colonies to combat poverty in
the slums, and appears to renounce a political critique
of this issue:

> If the world is ever to be saved, it will be saved by love . . .
> and then THIS world will be heaven . . . it will not be
> brought about by setting employed against employers,
> preaching a class war and persecuting blacklegs.[9]

These sentiments bring to mind Webb's remark about
Harkness's rejection of theory, and they also attest to a
wish, or even a belief, that social and political struggle
can be superseded. She declares her impatience with
contemporary political struggles such as the Dock Strike
because they do not produce the 'socialist millenium',
and she asserts a utopian belief in the power of human
love to bring people together and one day guide all
human actions. It seems that Harkness expected
socialism to provide an immediate, all-embracing
solution to the problems of late nineteenth century
Britain—her impatience for change was a feature
evident in SDF activity which Engels had criticized,
accusing the organization of adventurism and gullibility
in its relations with the London poor, leading up to the
1886 riots,[10]—and when the new order failed to
materialise she lost faith in her socialist vision. 'Faith'
and 'belief' are not casually used here, since as Webb
noted, Harkness never abandoned belief in a 'personal
adoration of Christ' throughout her years of socialist
agitation, and although her first three novels criticize
religious institutions, she retained respect for religious
people, particularly the Salvation Army, and an interest

in the suffering of Jesus Christ. Goode speculates that her 'involvement with socialism may have been emotive rather than thought out' and on the strength of available evidence this is a credible suggestion. Her fundamental commitment was to the poorest people in the cities, the 'class below the unskilled labourers: I mean the scum of our population that haunts the slums of our great cities',[11] and when socialist struggles seemed to have failed this section of the population, she turned her attention towards the organization which she perceived was most able to alleviate their misery and penury, the Salvation Army. Her interest in the work of the Army remained constant from this date onwards, but did not prevent her from writing what Sidney Webb described as 'a sensational *Tendenz Roman*' (socialist novel) in the *Women's Herald* about barmaids, which appeared in 1891–1892, under her pseudonym. This work was followed by years spent abroad, travelling in the British colonies and writing a number of books on India in the early twentieth century. In 1905 she published *George Eastmont: Wanderer*, a novel which dealt with disappointment with socialism, told through the character of an idealistic upper-class young man. The dedication to this novel reads:

> This book which contains the Writer's experience in the Labour Movement, and thoughts about it, is dedicated to the memory of His Eminence, Cardinal Manning, with whom the author was associated during the great dock strike of 1889.

Harkness returned to England, and wrote a novel about the Salvation Army in London during the war years, *A Curate's Promise: a story of Three Weeks* (Sept 14–Oct 5, 1917), which was published in 1921. There are no known details about her life after this date.

The decade of the 1880s was undoubtedly the period

when Harkness's novel writing powers were at their height, and her skill was intimately related to her engagement with the political, social and personal issues of working-class life in the cities. As the closing chapters of *Out of Work* reveal, when she moved out of this environment her narrative powers and incisive critical observation rapidly diminish.

Out of Work was written in the early years of controversy over the reception of French literary naturalism in Britain. Zola's *Germinal* was published here in 1885, and Harkness had read and been influenced by his work, referring to it briefly in *Out of Work* when describing the prison. 'That place needs a Zola to do it justice.' (p204) But Harkness's novel moves beyond the parameters of literary naturalism, achieving a style of documentary writing where the narrator intervenes throughout the narrative, commenting on and questioning orthodox representations of East End life. The story of Joseph Coney, the young carpenter who leaves his rural village when business declines, goes to London with £50 in his pocket to seek work and becomes one of the many thousands of impoverished, unemployed men and women who are despised and reviled for their misfortune, is narrated by a partisan observer. This observer is concerned to present a different East End story, one which deconstructs the familiar picture of self-induced degradation and offers a different version of reality: a reality which tells the story of East End poverty from 'below.' Engels had written that the attempts of the working class to recover 'their status as human beings belong to history and must therefore lay claim to a place in the domain of realism';[12] Harkness reinstates this class in her fiction. She gives it a presence and a voice through Jos Coney and the communities of slum dwellers amongst whom he lives. Coney is presented not as a single protagonist, but is a typical example of the casual poor. He comes into contact with many who share his plight, characters who, for all that they are part of the novel's meaning, usually remain anonymous. The narrator acts almost as interpreter, mediating between the East-End working class and the prospective middle-class readership, in a bid to disrupt complacent prejudices, suggesting at various points in the narrative that only political solutions can remedy chronic unemployment and poverty. The dock labourer, for example, is a man destroyed by lack of opportunities. 'He was one of the many people crushed out by our present competitive system. He might have been a statesman or a judge if he had been born in more favourable surroundings.' (p59) Thousands of workers are de-skilled by unemployment in an age of unrestrained competition. They become the anonymous army of casual labour at the dock gates, and Jos is driven into their ranks, having fallen out of 'the ranks of the great army that goes marching on, heedless of stragglers, whose commander-in-chief is *laissez-faire*.' (p120) And the Socialist speaker on Mile End Waste counsels his audience to help themselves by joining the class struggle against their oppressors. He promises 'Competition has had its day ... co-operation is the next step in the evolution of society' (p67)

The Queen's Jubilee (a celebration of the greatness of the British Empire) and the unemployed riots in Trafalgar Square (a reminder of the human cost of expansionist imperial power), two real incidents which occurred in 1887, provide the framework within which contemporary reality is examined. At the outset 'reporters were busy at work concocting stories of the royal progress. (p2) The narrator remarks that they would judiciously suppress accounts of 'the hisses which the denizens of the slums had mingled with faint applause' (p2) for Jubilee London is, after all, a god-fearing respectable place where Sunday church and chapel bells call on people to forget earth and think of

heaven. The satisfied calm of Sunday service at the
Wesleyan chapel is disturbed by earthly concerns in the
form of a rude interruption from a ragged, drink-
sodden, homeless man demanding to know whether the
godly preacher has ever been "ungry.' (p13) This man,
whose silence is bought for a penny from the minister,
represents the end result of poverty, starvation, unemployment and homelessness, he has been crushed by the
economic system and is reviled by the middle class
congregation.

The story which unfolds demonstrates the steady
process of decline which an honest working man experiences when he is faced with the same circumstances.
The East End poor are presented sympathetically. They
are not people with hereditary weaknesses (as Zola
typically made his characters) and although Jos becomes a drinker, following in the footsteps of his father,
this is a response to the stresses of his environment. In
addition, Jos is presented in a Christian frame of
reference, his initials J.C. are those of Jesus Christ, his
first name is Joseph and his profession is carpentry.
When the 'pretty Methodist' Polly Elwin breaks her
promise to marry him, she chooses the Wesleyan class
leader, William Ford instead. Ford, who works at the
Royal Mint, represents the bribe of silver and gold to
which Polly succumbs, and the symbolism of this
triangular affair is completed when Jos calls her 'a little
hypocrite' (p221) for making a false profession of
intention to marry him, then betraying him.

The Christian theme is employed at other points in
the narrative: the Socialist's speech includes criticism of
the clergy. 'They preach about the carpenter's Son to
congregations who would scorn to invite Jesus of
Nazareth to their grand parties' (p66); and at the close
of the novel the deaths of Jos and his faithful doss-house
friend, Squirrel, are accompanied by religious references. A clumsy symbolism is introduced in the scene of

Squirrel's suicide, but her death is placed in the context of a wider, necessary sacrifice, when the narrator intones the final words:

"'My God! My God! why hast thou forsaken me?'"
"'It is finished!'" (p268)

The references to the Christian story are incorporated into the narrative to sustain and support the argument for socialist action; and the picture of East End life which is constructed shows the alienation of the working class from other classes. It is conveyed through the social habits and ideology of Polly and her 'Methodist world' and is also perceptively examined in Jos and Polly's relationship. Polly is the daughter of lower middle class parents, her father is dead and her mother reigns with fierce religious bigotry over a household of foreign lodgers who provide the necessary income to allow her to employ a domestic servant and to maintain a quiet, genteel existence punctuated by weekly attendance at chapel and Sunday tea with 'Uncle' Cohen. She is opposed to Polly's engagement, and works steadily to undermine that relationship. Polly has absorbed her mother's social aspirations and ideals, and dreams of married life with Jos in a little house in Hackney: 'a little house with Venetian blinds in the windows, and a brass knocker on the door must, she imagined, have happy people inside it.' (p42) She wishes to escape from the blighted East End because 'people who live in Shoreditch, or St. George's-in-the-East are apt to be confounded with their poorer neighbours by the uninitated.' (p42) Her ambition is to become one of the 'respectable people, who pay their bills, go to chapel, and eat meat on Sunday', (p43) and she nurtures these desires whilst Jos steadily slides down the rigidly stratified East End social scale. His decline prevents him from visiting Polly, particularly after he is forced to abandon all hope of finding work as a carpenter and becomes a casual dock labourer. Just as his appearance and job debar him from Polly's society, so do his injuries prevent him from getting casual work at the docks until he is healthier. The narrator signals Jos's awareness of the importance of status and appearances after his first day at the docks: 'he looked like his mates, and they looked like him . . . he saw people turn away; he felt he had dropped to a lower level of things.' (p135)

Polly's recognition of the unbridgeable gulf between them occurs when she meets Jos in the street, after his night spent in prison following the Trafalgar Square riots. She recoils in shock and disgust from his worn-out, ragged physical appearance, and resorts to her mother's words in her rejection of him: 'I'm not going to marry you Joseph Coney, I'm going to marry a godly young man with a settled income.' (p221) She has submitted to the social attraction of a [regular monthly income] and the social appearances it can buy, in part to escape from her isolated and unhappy life at home. Like her mother, consciousness of social status suppresses any urge towards socialibity; she is unable to develop the friendship offered by her mother's domestic servant, Mary Anne, because of her concern to maintain the necessary social distance between them.

The only evidence of sociable relations is observed amongst the casual poor. The dockers live by the philosophy 'I help you and you help me because we've no place in society' (p129) and the doss-house poor 'shared scraps and lent halfpence.' (p153) In the doss-house Squirrel 'adopts' Jos and takes care of him when he is ill or drunk. For Jos, this relationship does not compromise his engagement to Polly because he views Squirrel as a temporary substitute-mother and friend, and even though Polly, too, reminds him of his mother, her respectable modesty also recalls his home, his past, and gives him hope because she contains the promise of a better future.

The Trafalgar Square riots are a significant public incident where different versions of reality compete. The tense and vivid accounts of the scene of confrontation— the class war in a public square—is interrupted by the narrator's leading questions:

> Was it true that the agitators were ''ungry' or was it false? . . . (were they) vagrants who wanted to play on the sympathies of the public, scum that must be allowed to die like dogs in the streets by order of the Political Economists? (p197)

The picture presented is one of large-scale police hostility and aggression, highlighted by specific incidents: Jos being batoned by a policeman for falling against him; Jos being arrested, to the accompaniment of cries of 'Shame' from the surrounding crowd; the actions of those men and women who offer themselves for arrest to the awaiting policemen: 'the huge constables, drawing themselves up to their full height said, "We cannot do it unless you assault us."' (p200) After depicting these incidents, the narrator is compelled to conclude,

> if more people had followed the example of those men and women, if it had *really* been a Bloody Sunday, the labour programme which is looming in the distance would now be before Parliament, Lord Salisbury and his party would ere this have vanished into nothingness. (p201)

Clearly regretting the failed courage of the rioters, Harkness counterposes their defeat with the devious manoeuvres of their enemies, who fabricate and mismanage evidence in court to perpetuate their version of events, and the class struggle promoted by the Socialist speaker is, it is implied, one which must be fought out in all areas of society.

Like many novels of social observation of its era, the conclusion of *Out of Work* is bleak and depressing because the working class experienced defeats in 1887.

Consequently Jos's death is both bitter and representative, and even death does not bring relief from conflicting representations, interpretations and judgements. 'The doctor said that his death must have been brought about by starvation ... the jury did not agree in their verdict, because a penny was found in his waistcoat pocket.' (p279)

NOTES

1. 'Engels to Margaret Harkness in London' in Marx, K. and Engels, F. *On Literature and Art* Moscow, 1976, Progress Publishers, pp89–92.
2. Goode, J. 'Margaret Harkness and the socialist novel' in Klaus, H.G. *The Socialist Novel in Britain* Sussex, 1982, Harvester, p57.
3. Kaspar, B. *Margaret Harkness, 'A City Girl'* Tubingen, 1984, Max Niemeyer Verlag. (German Text).
4. *The Diary of Beatrice Webb, Vol. 1: 1873–1892* edited by N. and J. Mackenzie, London, 1982, Virago in association with the London School of Economics and Political Science.
5. Kaspar's monograph includes what is known to be a comprehensive list of Harkness's published writing.
6. Law, J. 'Letter to the Editor', *Justice* 20/4/1889. p3.
7. Harkness, M.E. 'Letter to the Editor', *The Star* 25/9/1889. p4.
8. Harkness, M. 'Salvationists and Socialists', *Justice* 14/4/1888. p6.
9. Law, J. 'Salvation vs. Socialism—In Praise of General Booth', *Pall Mall Gazette* 21/10/1890. pp1–2.
10. Jones, S.G. *Outcast London* Harmondsworth, 1984, Penguin, 1st edn. 1971, p345.
11. Law, J. 'A year of My Life', *New Review* 5, 1891. p377.
12. Draft of an unfinished letter to Margaret Harkness cited in Kapp, Y. *Eleanor Marx. Vol. 2: The Crowded Years* London, 1979, Virago, p221.

TO

JOHN LAW

OF LAURISTON

" *Poverty is the parent of a thousand mental and moral evils. What is still worse, to be injured or oppressed, when habitual, lowers the whole tone of the character. One bad action leads to others, both in the agent himself, the bystanders, and in the sufferers. All bad qualities are strengthened by habit, and all vices and follies tend to spread. Intellectual defects generate moral, and moral intellectual; and every intellectual or moral defect generates others, and so on without end.*"

JOHN STUART MILL.

CONTENTS.

PART I.

CONTENTS.

PART II.

OUT OF WORK.

PART I.

CHAPTER I.

A WESLEYAN CHAPEL.

IT was the day after the Queen's visit to the
East End.   Whitechapel was gay with flags.
Mile End had coloured banners, and festoons
of red, yellow, green, and blue paper flowers
"all along the line."   About seventeen hours
earlier Her Majesty had been enthusiastically
welcomed by crowds of West End visitors at
the London Hospital and the great breweries.
Cheers from the lungs of medical students still

echoed in the air ; scents from the pockethand-
kerchiefs of brewers' wives and doctors'
daughters rose upwards.   Reporters were busy
at work concocting stories of the royal progress
through the East End for the Monday papers ;
artists were preparing for the illustrated weekly
papers pictures of Whitechapel as it may
possibly appear in the Millennium.   No one
would speak about the hisses which the
denizens of the slums had mingled with faint
applause as Her Majesty neared her destina-
tion ; no one would hint that the crowd about
the Palace of Delight had had a sullen, ugly
look which may a year or so hence prove
dangerous.   The ladies on their way to the
Queen's Hall, who had leant back languidly in
their carriages, heedless of ragged men, hungry
women, and little dirty children, the *blasé*
frequenters of Hyde Park and the clubs, who
had glanced carelessly at the people as they
accompanied their wives and daughters to the
People's Palace, would be quoted by reporters
as philanthropic persons intent on ministering
to the poor by the unction of their presence,
and represented by the artists as so many
unselfish ladies and gentlemen, who had given

up an afternoon's pleasure-hunting in order to gratify the eyes of under-paid men and over-worked women by their shining hats and charming bonnets.

It was Sunday morning, about eleven o'clock, so the bells of churches and chapels were calling upon people to forget earth and think of heaven.

Some way down a street at the back of the Commercial Road, the doors of a Wesleyan chapel stood wide open. A man, dressed in black, was on the stone steps which led to the entrance. He had a book in his hand, and his thumb marked the third page. He was watching the congregation, waiting to conduct a stranger to a place, if any stranger came to join in "morning worship," to supply Bibles and Wesleyan hymn-books, and to keep watch over the younger portion of the congregation who might chance to bring nuts and oranges into chapel.

The chapel was square, and built of brick. Its walls were whitewashed; its doors were painted black. Between the doors, on the wall which faced the stone steps, was an almanack, with Mr. Wesley's portrait in the centre, and pictures of saintly men like Watson and Fletcher at the four corners of it.

There is, said the almanack, only one condition previously required of those who wish to become Methodists; namely, "a desire to flee from the wrath to come, and be saved from their sins." Sinners who conform to this receive a ticket of membership; they are enrolled as members of the Methodist Society, which is "a company of men having the form, and seeking the power, of godliness; united in order to pray together, to receive the word of exhortation, and to watch over one another in love, that they may help each other to work out their salvation."

The man who stood at the entrance of the chapel was a steward, and well known to the congregation. They greeted him as they passed, laughing and talking, through the door, to take their places in pews with narrow knee-boards and neat wooden boxes which held Bibles and hymn-books.

The outside of the chapel was ugly; the inside was hideous. A gallery ran along the walls, north, south, and east, halfway between the floor and the ceiling. West was the organ-loft, with tiers of seats for the singers. Beneath the organ-loft was the pulpit, furnished with armchairs, cushions, and footstools. Two flights of steps, covered with bright blue carpet, led down from the pulpit into the body of the chapel. Beneath the pulpit were the Communion Table, the Font, and a door communicating with the vestry.

The chapel had been built to hold five hundred people, but that Sunday morning only two hundred men, women, and children had come to worship in it. These two hundred formed a well-fed, well-dressed little company, cheerful and contented, as people ought to be who are in a "state of grace," who know that, whatever may happen to the unsaved, their own souls are safe.

Perhaps this feeling of security in some measure accounted for the careless behaviour of the Methodists, the nodding and smiling they indulged in after a prayer had been said, and places had been found in Bibles and hymn-books. People who are on good terms with the Deity, and accustomed to treat Him with fraternal intimacy, may well dispense with the bowing and scraping which seem good in the eyes of Puseyites and Catholics. Besides, the nonchalance about the souls of others which Mr. Wesley's doctrines palliate, relieves the saved from undue responsibility concerning those who refuse to flee from the wrath to come, who, being born in sin and shapen in wickedness, must be left to perish.

" If there be any among us who observe not the rules of our faith and practice, who habitually break any of them, let it be made known unto them who watch over that soul, as they that must give account," says Mr. Wesley. "We will admonish him of the error of his ways: we will bear with him for a season. But then, if he repent not, he hath no more place among us. *We have delivered our own souls.*"

Presently, among this tidy, self-complacent little congregation, appeared a man in tattered clothes and battered-in hat. He passed the steward, who looked suspiciously at him, as though his pocket might contain gunpowder and his hat hold dynamite. As he walked into the chapel, men stared at him and women drew away their dresses. He went to a seat close under the pulpit. There he stood for a minute. His trousers were made of fustian,

and tied under the knee with pieces of rope.
His long, loose brown coat was patched with
sacking, bits of leather, cotton, and cloth. His
dirty shirt had no wristbands, no collar, only
frayed ends of cotton and shreds of print, which
hung about his arms and neck. Round his
throat he wore a bit of red flannel, which he
had most likely found in some dustheap, and
on his feet were old boots, which he had probably
received as a present from a kind-hearted ven-
dor of rags in Houndsditch. His face had a
sodden look, as though he were hopeless of life
and callous of his appearance. His eyes were
swollen by drink; his hands trembled; his legs
shook. He sat down and buried his head on
his arms, so the steward who had followed him
into chapel did not trouble to offer him Bible
or hymn-book.

Ten minutes later the vestry door opened,
and the ministers of the circuit came through
the rails which enclosed the Communion Table.
They mounted the staircase that led to the
pulpit. The elder, Mr Meek, ran quickly up
the steps. He was followed more sedately
by Mr. Stry, the subordinate minister. Mr.
Meek's movements were animated by a buoyant

spirit; but Mr. Stry had not found his experience of life tally with his convictions; he was dyspeptic.

The two ministers had possibly been chosen to work together on account of the perfect contrast which they presented to the eyes, if not to the minds, of their congregation. Mr. Meek was short, broad, and stout, with dark hair parted low on his forehead, and thick black whiskers and moustache covering his mouth and cheeks. His eyes twinkled, and, but for the presence of Mr. Stry, it is just possible that he might have been guilty of making puns in the pulpit. His prayers were thanksgivings, praises of the Almighty Who had made this world such a pleasant place to live in, Who had promised to convert earthly joy into heavenly bliss. He thanked God for "creation, preservation, and all the blessings ·of this life," and above all for the free gift of salvation; namely, of eternal happiness, which His servants had only gratefully to accept without exerting themselves much to get it.

Mr. Stry was tall, thin, and angular. His face was marked by smallpox. His sandy hair grew very upright, his sandy beard was cut in a sharp point. He had neither whiskers nor moustache, so the curious twitching of his upper lip was visible, giving a clue to his dyspeptic temperament. Mr. Stry did not flatter the Deity. He reminded Him of His duties, and implored Him to pour out His wrath on all but His chosen people, to punish all save the elect. The wickedness of the nations, the depravity of human nature, were the chief topics of his sermons; and entreaties to the Almighty that He would not forget justice in mercy, or spare the wicked, formed the staple of his prayers, mixed with allusions to the lost, Satan, and eternal punishment.

Mr. Stry seated himself in an armchair, and Mr. Meek having taken his place before a large Bible on the reading desk, and smiled upon the gallery above and the pews beneath, gave out a hymn, which he read verse by verse, before the congregation began to sing it.

> "God, the offended God, most high,
> Ambassadors to rebels sends,
> His messengers His place supply,
> And Jesus begs us to be friends.
> While the wicked are confounded,
> Doomed to flames and woe unbounded,
> Call *me* with Thy saints surrounded,"
> O God of love!

The man in rags did not stand up with the congregation to sing the hymn; but when it was finished he raised his head and looked round for a minute. Then he buried his head on his arms again. He was sitting close to the pulpit, and the big Bible hid him from view, so Mr. Meek did not know that a stranger was present. The minister only saw familiar faces, faces of people whose joys and sorrows he was well acquainted with, as he placed his fat right hand over his fat left wrist, and offered up a thanksgiving to the Deity when the hymn was finished.

Mr. Stry read chapters from the Bible, and gave notice of meetings to be held during the week, also of the times fixed for classes, and details concerning a tent mission and the next lovefeast. Some more hymns were sung; another prayer was said, during which the congregation ejaculated "Praise the Lord!" and "Amen." Then Mr. Meek gave out a text, and began to talk confidentially with his hearers upon a subject which had engaged his thoughts during the past week. He bent over the pulpit with a smile on his face. Suddenly the smile vanished, and he drew back. He had seen the man in rags; or rather, he had caught sight of a tattered coat and some grisly hair, and a figure bowed so low that the head would have touched the knees, but for the black hands which supported it.

The minister recovered himself in a minute, and fixing his eyes on the gallery repeated the text:—

"And even as they did not like to retain God in their knowledge, God gave them over to a reprobate mind, to do those things which are not convenient."

"Dear friends," said the minister, "my mind has lately been much exercised on the subject of sceptics. I am convinced, I know it to be true, that a man without a creed is a man, *must* be a man, without principles for practical godliness; yet I am bound to admit that I often come across men possessing no religion, men having no creed, who apparently live unselfish, upright lives, who appear to be good fathers, husbands, and citizens. I have searched the Holy Scriptures for an answer to these things, knowing that a high and complete morality is impossible without faith in God, and

that salvation can only be obtained by belief in
original sin, Divine inspiration, eternal re-
wards and punishments, and the other doctrines
of the christian religion. And I have been
vouchsafed an answer to my questioning ; for
I have found that it does not do to judge
sceptics as individuals. We must read the fate
of unbelievers in the history of nations. The
natural man may appear good when we see
him isolated from his fellows ; but directly
unbelievers become a power in a nation, we see
them in their real colours, drunkards, blasphem-
ers, given up to a reprobate mind, doing those
things which are not convenient. Without
belief in God and eternal life a man is not
capable of real godliness ; the appearance of it
may be there, but do not believe in appearances. The strength of morality is God ; and
a nation without God is sure to become like
Sodom and Gomorrah, my friends, like Sodom
and Gomorrah. As a proof of this you have
but to look around you. Behold England
seated high above the nations of the earth,
behold our beloved country famed for its
strength, honoured for its wealth, envied for
its great possessions ! Our princes are clothed

in scarlet. Our Queen rules over a kingdom upon which the sun never sets, she is Empress of India, Protectress of Burmah, Benefactress of Egypt, and Royal Mother of the Colonies. All these things have been given us because we are a God-fearing nation. The smile of God is upon us, because Sunday by Sunday our thanksgivings and praises ascend to Him as incense. So He vouchsafes us His blessing. He fills us with corn and wine. He——"

"Sir," asked a voice, "'ave you ever been 'ungry?"

It was the ragged man who put the question. He was standing up where Mr. Meek could see him, and his red, inflamed eyes were fixed on the minister's complacent countenance. His voice was deep and gruff; it had no music in it.

"'Ave you ever been 'ungry?" he repeated, determined to have an answer, "'ungry?"

"I do not know what pain means in that sense, my friend," said Mr. Meek, with a stutter. "I was speaking of corn and wine figuratively, you know—ah! figur-a-tive-ly."

"'Ave you ever been 'ungry?" the man persisted.

Mr. Stry slid down the pulpit steps and went to the ragged questioner, who, after a few words, took up his hat and went out of chapel. He looked neither to the right nor to the left, as he walked between the pews full of astonished, indignant Methodists. His face had a look of dogged, hopeless wretchedness, which he could only shake off in the gin-shop. He went to a public-house directly he was outside the chapel, and waited at the door, with his hat over his eyes, and his fingers clasped tightly on the penny with which Mr. Stry had silenced his questions.

The panegyric of the godly nation fell flat after the ragged man had departed. Mr. Meek tried to revive his eloquence, but a weight seemed to hang on his tongue, as he spoke of the Queen's Jubilee, the Royal thanksgiving in Westminster Abbey, the glory and the pageant with which the godly nation was about to celebrate a prosperous period of English history. He fell back on the wickedness of unbelievers, and painted a gloomy picture of England's fate if unbelief ever obtruded its Gorgon head among us. He begged his congregation to live worthy of their calling, worthy of the Gospel, worthy of their country, worthy of the Lord, worthy of His kingdom of glory, with longsuffering and joyfulness, in the unity of the spirit and the bond of peace.

The school children grew restless, the singers fidgeted with their books, and every one seemed relieved when the minister finished his discourse and gave out the final hymn,—

> "Righteous God! Whose vengeful phials,
> All our fears and thoughts exceed.
> Big with woes and fiery trials,
> Hanging, breaking o'er our head.
> While Thou visitest the nations,
> *Thy selected people spare.*
> Arm our cautioned souls with patience,
> Fill our humbled hearts with prayer."
>
> Alleluia!

CHAPTER II.

AMONG the Methodists, but almost last of all to leave the chapel, were a mother and daughter who had occupied seats in the gallery facing the pulpit. For twenty years Mrs. Elwin had sat in the same pew Sunday after Sunday; and for fifteen years, at least, her daughter had accompanied her. Polly Elwin could remember the day when she first climbed the steps to the gallery, holding on to her father's finger, and stood on a footstool staring at the strange scene about her. She could recollect sitting with the school children to the left of the organ loft, and she could recall the Sunday on which she (dressed in black) had placed mourning cards in the pews of her mother's friends, cards with black edges, which said that her father had gone to his rest, and that henceforth she and her mother must live and work by themselves. She knew each member of the congregation by name, and could say who had been christened, who had been married, and who had been converted during the last two years without making a single mistake. Moreover, she kept a mental register of all the new bonnets and dresses, and silently convicted their wearers, as the case might be of slovenliness or extravagance. She partook regularly of the lovefeasts, was a member of the Extension of Methodism Society, collected money for the Worn-out Ministers, and Ministers' Widows' Auxiliary Fund, and seldom failed in class, unless she was really ill. She never stayed away from chapel because she had a headache. As she followed her mother that morning her eyes were fixed on the ground. It was a habit of hers, that looking down. The habit suited her face, it was so modest. But when she raised her eyes one felt disappointed. Her eyes were blue and small, with light brown lashes, very like her mother's eyes, but less keen and determined. There were signs about her that both face and figure would resemble Mrs. Elwin twenty years hence; although now the soft pink cheeks were

2

round and dimpled, the white throat had no hard lines about it, the light brown hair lay wavy and thick on her forehead, and the small nose and mouth had not developed into hardness. The neat red dress and black jacket fitted her slight figure, the black straw hat trimmed with red velvet suited her complexion; and all three increased the effect produced by her drooping eyelids.

Mrs. Elwin's figure was plump. Her face had what is called "a comely look." The roses had matured rather than faded in her cheeks, for a bright colour made her appear ten years younger than she really was, and people often told her "we took you and your daughter for sisters." Her shrewd blue eyes could grow soft sometimes, for instance, when the minister was paying her a visit. Her mouth was drawn in, and the upper lip fell at the corner, perhaps from the want of teeth she had had extracted, perhaps from the struggle of life, a struggle in which she had come to the front soon after her marriage with Mr. Elwin. (Marriage generally results in the survival of the fittest; which fact cannot be grumbled at, since it is a law of existence that the weakest must go to the wall, and a dogma, established by experience, that mind rules matter, no matter how strong matter may be.) Mrs. Elwin wore a purple silk dress, one of those old-fashioned colours that put to shame our modern tints ; and she carried an Indian shawl on her shoulders, fastened at the neck with a large brooch. The brooch contained a portrait of "the late lamented Mr. Elwin." So she called him.

The mother and daughter walked slowly out of chapel, a little behind the rest of the congregation, for Mrs. Elwin did not " hold " with gossip after " Divine worship." Moreover, " she kept herself to herself ; " and it was a favourite question among the Methodists *why* Mrs. Elwin fancied herself better than other people, a frequently repeated wish that she should one day learn "those who think much of themselves are generally but lightly esteemed by their neighbours."

Polly nodded to one or two friends, but Mrs. Elwin took little notice of anybody as she passed through the gates and went into an open space beside the chapel. Here she was wont "to take the air " for a few minutes before she returned home ; a luxury she could indulge in because she kept a servant, and consequently was not obliged to hurry back to her house directly the sermon was finished. She seated herself on a bench to admire the stunted shrubs and sickly looking plants, to point out the lilacs which were beginning to put forth thin bunches of flowers, and the laburnum hanging over the fountain in the centre of a grass plot. A young woman passed by carrying a large bunch of rhubarb; and Mrs. Elwin remarked that "those sort of folks never will learn how wrong it is to buy victuals on the Sabbath." An old man tottered by, the inmate of a workhouse, and Mrs. Elwin shook her head over him, saying, "It's wrong enough to drink on weekdays, but to drink on the Lord's day is downright wicked." Then the mother and daughter discussed the ragged man who had disturbed the minister, and agreed that the steward ought not to have given him a seat in chapel.

"Considering all that's done for those sort of folks, it's a wonder they ain't better," said Mrs. Elwin. "But there, I do believe if Queen Victoria herself were to come among them, they'd take no account of her; they'd go on drinking and fighting, they'd take no notice,"

"I thought she looked tired yesterday," remarked Polly, "and Jos said she looked cross."

"Joseph Coney don't know what he's talking about," answered her mother sharply. "It's hard on a woman of her years to go gadding about. She'll be glad when this Jubilee business is over and done with, so she can keep quiet."

The colour deepened in Polly's cheeks. But she did not look at her mother. She remained silent, with her eyes fixed on the ground.

A clock struck one.

"Uncle Cohen will be waiting for us," said Mrs. Elwin ; "it's time to go home."

They went through back streets, full of trucks covered with unwholesome looking fishes, fishes whose names are unknown in polite society, whose huge heads and minute bodies are only appreciated in Whitechapel. Tubs of pickled cucumbers stood on movable tables, and by these were stalls covered with cockles, pigs' feet, and large tins full of eel-broth. The inhabitants of the slums were holding a Sunday picnic, indulging in dainty East End dishes, which they bought at a low price, and washed down with draughts from a neighbouring public-house.

"Hokey-pokey! who'll buy it?" cried a man. He was wheeling a tin down the middle of the road, a tin full of ice, cut in squares and wrapt in paper. The ragged boys and girls flocked round him, for they enjoyed ice-cream more than sour cucumbers, and hokey-pokey seldom made its appearance on week-days, but always came on Sundays to furnish a dessert to the picnic, an "end-up" to the out-door repast. How the dirty little feet danced! How the grimy little hands clapped! "Hokey-pokey! who'll buy it?" opened doors as if by magic, and brought longing faces to the windows. More than one small child crept into a public-house to plead for a penny out of "daddy's" pocket; and when a kick was the answer, a cry of pain mixed with bitter disappointment was heard, as the hokey-pokey man disappeared round a corner into another street.

Mrs. Elwin was so much accustomed to these sights, she scarcely heaved a sigh as she passed the stalls and the people. But when she reached the road her house stood in, and caught sight of some children inside the gate which led to her front door, she quickened her steps. The little miscreants were chasing sunbeams on the clean white steps; a most innocent amusement, but one which left traces of dirty fingers and black toes, to say nothing of the mud they thought fit to throw at the dancing spots, spots which eluded their hands and feet, at which they spat.

"This is the way you keep the Sabbath, is it?" cried Mrs. Elwin, boxing the ears of a boy, and catching hold of a girl by the hair of her head. "Where do you think you'll go to when you die, you bad, wicked children? Have you no mothers to teach you nothing?"

She stopped, out of breath, and as the children escaped, she turned to vent her wrath upon her maidservant, who had opened the door while she was dealing with the little Sabbath-breakers.

"Mary Anne," she exclaimed, "it's all your fault. The many times I've told you not to leave that gate open! I've spoken till I'm tired of speaking. Do you hear me?"

There was little doubt that Mary Anne heard Mrs. Elwin, but her look of indifference gave reason to suppose that she was deaf or stupid. She turned away, leaving the enraged lady to recover from what she called "Missus's

Sunday temper." She followed Polly, who had gone upstairs to take off her hat and jacket in a small bedroom at the top of the house. While the pretty Methodist smoothed the soft fair hair on her forehead, Mary Anne threw herself upon the bed, and rocked her body backwards and forwards without speaking.

"What's the matter?" inquired Polly.

"I'm sick hon't," said the little maidservant.

"Sick of what?"

"Sick of bein' myself. It's Mary Hanne here, and Mary Hanne there; it's nothing but Mary Hanne heverywhere. I wish I wasn't Mary Hanne. I wish I was hanybody helse."

"You shouldn't talk like that," replied Polly, still looking into the glass and smoothing her hair. "You should be content with the place God has put you in, and not give way to wicked feelings."

"It's hall very well for you to talk," responded Mary Anne. "You can go to see the Queen and heverything. You promised you'd get back yesterday in time for me to see the hold lady, and you didn't do it. You was along with your sweetheart."

"I tried my best to get back," said Polly;

"the crowd was so thick, Jos told me I mustn't be in a hurry. It wasn't my fault."

"Mary Anne!" called Mrs. Elwin.

"Hat it hagain," groaned Mary Anne, slowly getting off the bed, "hat it halways. Oh dear! I wish I wasn't Mary Hanne. I wish I was you, I wish I wasn't meself."

"Mary Anne! Mary Anne!" cried Mrs. Elwin.

"Mary Hanne! Mary Hanne!" mocked the little maidservant. "I'm a-comin', missus. Them haddocks hall right."

She stretched herself, and turned to show Polly a boot with a hole in it.

"A needle stuck in my foot this morning," she said, "look how my foot's a-bleedin'. I guess if missus do let me hout to-night, I can't walk. It hurts hawful when I walks about."

Then she left Polly to meditate on the depravity of girls like herself, and went downstairs to dish up dinner in a small dark hole called "the kitchen." She did nearly all the housework,—no light task, as Mrs. Elwin took in lodgers,—and she had at least ten rooms to do, and fifteen people to attend to. Mrs. Elwin superintended; Polly did needlework. So Mary

Anne was everybody's servant. She scrubbed and cooked, she swept and dusted, she made beds and carried up water, she sometimes gave the rooms what she called "a turn-hout." Half an hour before she went to bed she dressed herself and washed her face; the rest of the day she wore rags, and had her hair in curl papers. Her supreme delight was to uncurl her hair just before bedtime, wash her hands and face, put on a clean apron, and sit down for what she called "half an hour's quiet." During those half hours she read dirty dog-eared novelettes which she found lying about the lodgers' bedrooms. In these she learnt that a haughty smile had curled Lord Mount Stevens' aristocratic lip, as he turned to Lady Gwendoline, saying, "This is too much." And that Lady Gwendoline had trembled like an aspen leaf, while Lord Mount Stevens crushed her lover's letter in his lordly fingers; that the blue veins had swollen on Lady Violet's snow-white forehead, and she had tapped her slender foot upon the velvet carpet, when Lord Randolph pleaded in dulcet tones the cause of her discarded lover; that the Marquis de Quincey had left his ancestral mansion with a sardonic smile, and had gone forth to become the prince of *roués*, because his proud old father had refused to let him graft the gardener's daughter upon the family tree. Afterwards Mary Anne dreamt of lords and ladies on her little hard bed, until she heard Mrs. Elwin screaming,

"It's five o'clock. Are you going to lie there all day? Get up, directly!"

Poor Mary Anne!

She had a brother somewhere in some workhouse, and a mother who ten years ago had gone on tramp, and never come back again. Mrs. Elwin had taken her from an aunt, and kept her because she worked like a galley-slave, and was strong as a horse. Her short stout figure seemed made to carry buckets, and her round red face showed that people *can* live on bread and scrape, with scarcely a glimpse of daylight. Her life had one advantage, at any rate, it left room for daydreams and hallucinations. Mary Anne firmly believed that she would have been perfectly happy, if it had pleased God to place her in aristocratic surroundings; and no doubt this delusion will remain with her always, even after she has married the butcher's boy, and settled down to have six children.

She dished up dinner—that is to say, she carried upstairs to the " parlour," a large saucepan full of boiled haddock, which she emptied on to a dish, and another saucepan full of potatoes, into which the company present plunged their forks as she walked round the table. Three people were there for dinner, Mrs. Elwin, her daughter, and a Jew, an elderly man, with crisp grey hair, long nose, and narrow eyes, named Cohen. At the door stood a red-haired youth, a lodger, who was complaining that his room was infested with mice, rousing Mrs. Elwin's indignation by suggesting a mouse-trap.

" I tell you there isn't a hole in the room. If you saw a mouse, young man, it came down the chimney, and it's at London Bridge by this time," said the landlady.

" I saw three mice all at once," the red-haired youth told her.

" Lor', that's nothin'," remarked Mary Anne. " We've rats in the kitchen. They come a-kickin' and a-jumpin' over my bed."

" Mind your own business," said her mistress.

' I'll send the cat up to your room to-morrow, young man.   Good-morning."

The " parlour" was a comfortable little room, with painted walls and large cupboards.   Wax flowers, covered with glass shades, adorned the mantel-piece.   Mrs. Elwin had made those flowers before she was married, and kept them as relics of her spinster-days ; reminiscences of maidenhood, immortalised in red roses and white lilies.   Two oil paintings faced one another on the walls, showing Mr. and Mrs. Elwin as they had been shortly after their marriage.   Both had rosy cheeks, glassy blue eyes, shining brown hair, and open mouths. They smiled on one another lover-wise ; and it is wonderful to think of the many matrimonial squabbles they had witnessed with perfect equanimity during the five-and-twenty years of the Elwins' matrimonial experiences.

Above the bookshelf was the skeleton of a cat, the best mouser Mrs. Elwin had ever possessed,—so good that she had lived entirely on mice, to say nothing of the rats with which she had fought many a gallant fight, and come off victorious.   Mrs. Elwin often looked at the skeleton, and sighed for the like of that dead pussy she would never see again, and the mice seemed to know it, said Mrs. Elwin.

The bookshelf held Methodist literature, and prizes Polly had won at school. From it Mrs. Elwin took down a volume every Sunday afternoon ; and over it she dozed, for on Sunday she indulged in a bottle of stout. With such a book on her knee she tried to convert the Jew Cohen, who called himself a sceptic. (How it came to pass that Mrs. Elwin allowed such a dangerous person inside her home will be explained presently.) A big horse-hair sofa was opposite the fireplace ; two armchairs, stood like sentinels by the hearthrug ; the Family Bible had a place between the windows ; the piano, on which Polly could play " God save the Queen," " The last Rose of Summer," and hymn tunes with one finger, occupied all the space between the bookshelf and the fireplace.

Directly dinner was over, Mrs. Elwin pushed her chair away from the table, Polly went upstairs, Cohen (Uncle Cohen they called him) seated himself in one of the armchairs, and lighted a pipe. He kept a small shop not far from Mrs. Elwin's house. He had been a friend of the late lamented Mr. Elwin. The friendship of these two men dated before the latter's marriage; and from that time Cohen had come there to dinner, because he was a bachelor, and had, as Mrs. Elwin said, no home to speak of, only a shop.

He did not pay for his dinner, but he was supposed to repay the hospitality shown to him by various presents, such as a goose at Christmas, an occasional bottle of wine, a silk dress for Mrs. Elwin when he came across a good bargain, and—after Polly made her appearance —"gifts to the little 'un." It was then he became Uncle Cohen. He was devoted to Polly. If his old bachelor heart could have been dissected that afternoon, a curious history would have been the result; one of parental, fraternal, and loverlike feelings, mixed with awe and admiration for that member of the other sex he had seen growing, developing from a tiny, helpless creature into a pretty young woman. She had sat on his knee as a baby, and now he often wished those days back again, for then he had felt her small hands on his face, and had been able to give her as many kisses as sugar-plums. But as years went on only sugar-

plums were accepted, kisses were refused, because "Uncle Cohen's beard is so rough;"
and now she treated him as an old fogey, to
be teased and laughed at for his bachelor
habits.

His shop was a wonderful place. Above the
door hung a placard, which promised easy
shaving, clean hair-cutting, painless dentistry,
and the very best tobacco, to all who entered
in. The window showed razors and strops,
cosmetics and pomatums, and instruments for
stopping and extracting teeth. Uncle Cohen
did not believe in new-fashioned dentistry. He
talked of the good old days when a man lay
down on the floor, and the dentist knelt on his
chest to get a good grip. He used a screw
that twisted, a sort of funnel into which he put
the tooth before he began to twist, which he
turned round and round until the tooth came
out. A sharp pull with tweezers he thought
unscientific, because it sometimes left bits behind. His funnel brought the fangs clean
away. He had a drawer full of extracted
teeth, specimens of which he exhibited in the
window.

Hair-cutting was his chief business. This

he performed before two long narrow looking-glasses. Between these glasses hung a picture of Mr. Gladstone's head, beneath which he had written—

> " Heads of great men all remind us
> We can make our heads sublime,
> And, departing, leave behind us
> Headprints on the sands of time."

This was the only literary composition he had ever indulged in, and he was proud of it. It showed, he said, what he might have accomplished if he had had time to become a poet.

Cosmetics he made himself. His *chef-d'œuvre*, the Mary Elwin cosmetic, promised to remove spots, soften the skin, and beautify the complexion of the fair sex. He sold it with grim jests, and never advised Polly to try it. Jewesses bought it, young women whose beauty fades much quicker than does that of their English sisters.

They also purchased his hairwash, which promised a quick crop of hair to those who sell their locks in the hair-market. He made wigs for these Jewesses, which looked almost as well as, if not better than, their own hair,

in the eyes of Jewish lovers. The East End
Jew has a keen sense of business. He does
not fall in love until he has considered his
future wife's capacity for making money, not
the least of which is a head capable of supply-
ing extra tresses to West End ladies.

Uncle Cohen had many theories about the
hair-business. He examined heads (scalps, he
called them), and diagnosed their case on principles of his own which may be true, as no
one has yet established a hair-theory, at least
not one at all generally accepted or known to
the public. Polly's hair was his great delight.
It showed, he said, what hair *could* be, and
was an encouragement.

Uncle Cohen had shaken off the shackles of
his religion ; he did not attend synagogue or
keep Passovers. He was a sceptic. But he
was open to conviction, so he was admitted
inside a Methodist house. That he would be
one day converted Mr. Elwin had been convinced, because he was by no means bigoted,
only indifferent. Mrs. Elwin worked at his
conversion every Sunday, and prayed for him
during the week, as she was bound to do by
the instructions of Mr. Wesley, while there was

any hope. And the fact that Uncle Cohen had a nice little sum of money put by in the bank, which he must leave some day to somebody, made his conversion a pleasure, as well as a duty, perhaps.

When Polly came downstairs again, she found her mother, whose mind was still exercised on the subject of mice, arguing with Uncle Cohen, trying to convince him of design and purpose made manifest to us by indisputable facts.

"Never tell me there isn't some one what puts thoughts into us just as He puts ways and habits into dumb beasts," Mrs. Elwin was saying. "Look at cats! They'll eat the whole of a mouse, head, tail, and every thing, but they'll only eat the forequarters of a rat."

"Why?" interrupted Uncle Cohen.

"Why? Because a cat knows the hindquarters of rats are poison, of course," replied Mrs. Elwin. "Don't you know that?"

"I'm not sure," began Uncle Cohen. But he stopped short in his remark, and said, "Are they really! Well, who'd have thought *that?*"

Mrs. Elwin smoothed her silk dress, and turned over a page of Mr. Wesley's sermons with complacence. It was not easy to convert a sceptic. So much the greater glory when the feat was accomplished.

"Where are you going?" she asked Polly.

"To meet Jos," the girl answered.

"Has Joseph Coney got any work yet?" inquired Uncle Cohen.

"Work!" exclaimed Mrs. Elwin, "I wish he had. I don't know what's come over young men nowadays. When the late lamented Mr. Elwin came courting, young men had plenty to do. It's their idle habits, I take it. Don't tell me there isn't work to be had, if young men care to do it."

"What time will you be back, Polly?"

"Before chapel, mother. May I bring Jos in to tea?"

"No; I won't have him. If I'd my way, you'd stay at home. I wonder he has the face to come courting."

Polly made no reply. She slipped quietly out of the room, and a few minutes later the front door slammed after her. Uncle Cohen walked to the window, and watched her going up the street. Mrs. Elwin turned Mr. Wesley's sermons upside down on her knee, and put a pocket-handkerchief over her face. These somnific signs Uncle Cohen was not slow to interpret. He took up his hat, and went back to his shop.

CHAPTER III.

VICTORIA PARK.

POLLY walked to the end of the street in which her mother's house stood, and turned to the left. There she saw a young man standing by the corner of Cannon Street, that leads into the Whitechapel Road. His back was towards her, his face was towards some flower-girls, who were inviting him to buy roses at a penny a-piece. He wore a neat suit of clothes, which (so one could easily see) had been made in the country. His black billy-cock was rather the worse for wear. As he took off his hat, and wiped his forehead with a red cotton pocket-handkerchief, one noticed that his brown hair stood upright, short and sharp, on his head. It showed no parting. Men of his class often dispense with partings; they wear their hair on end, cropped close to the skin. One does not see this sort of hair-dressing in the fashionable parts of London, but it is not unbecoming ; so no doubt some day one of the gentlemen at æsthetic Toynbee Hall, or ascetic Oxford House, will adopt it, and set the fashion in the West End. There was nothing remarkable about this young man's appearance. He was of middle height ; his shoulders were of normal breadth ; his chest was in proportion with the rest of his body ; his hands were long and narrow, with nervous-looking fingers ; his neck and face were sunburnt, so was his forehead up to the line at which his hat covered it ; his features were regular ; his chin slanted back ; he wore no beard, no whiskers, only a small brown moustache, which hid his upper lip, and which he had a nervous habit of biting. His eyes were deep-set, grey, with large pupils.

He looked as most young men of his class look, until one has time to recognise their individuality ; only, if an intelligent observer had come across him when he was roused out of his everyday existence, the intelligent observer would have cogitated over those eyes of his, and speculated as to his past—and his future.

The same intelligent observer, seeing him that Sunday afternoon, would have noticed something about his appearance that had nothing to do with his character, further than as an environment that might modify it in some directions and transform it in others. The flesh of his face was falling away, and by so doing was leaving the skin loose, ready to expand again, when a supply of food allowed it to be expanded. His face showed the first signs of starvation—signs easily interpreted by one who has studied the painful science of keeping alive on next-to-nothing, but never understood by those who receive their daily bread without effort or consideration. The intelligent observer would quickly have seen by his appearance that the young man had had no Sunday dinner, and would have suspected that for some days past dinners had been with him wishes incapable of realisation.

The young man shook his head at the flower-girls. Then, suddenly having caught sight of his coat-sleeves, which were frayed at the edges, he put his hand in his pocket. He produced a penny, and having received a red rose in exchange for it, he stuck the flower in his button-hole. The flower-girl watched him, and gave him a pin to fasten it with. She would have pinned it for him, only at that minute he felt a hand on his arm, and turning round he exclaimed,

" Polly ! "

" Jos ! " said the pretty Methodist.

They walked away together towards the Whitechapel Road ; and there, having mounted a red tramcar, they sat down on the top of it, side by side, hand in hand, without speaking.

East End people do a good deal of silent love-making, by signs and movements, tongue-tied. Polly and Jos had settled the day before that they would spend Sunday afternoon in Victoria Park, so they remained speechless until the tramcar had passed into Cambridge Street.

Then Polly asked,

" Jos, have you got any work yet ? "

" No," answered Jos.

They relapsed into silence, and their thoughts went in very different directions.

Polly thought of the changed look on the faces of the people, for as the tramcar left

Whitechapel, and drew near to Hackney, she saw fathers and mothers with smartly dressed babies, young women in their Sunday clothes, and young men who had had a bath, all going towards Victoria Park. The roads presented quite a gay appearance when she followed Jos down the tramcar steps, and walked with him up a street lined with neat little houses. A little house in Hackney was, it seemed to Polly, a Paradise. A little house with venetian blinds in the windows, and a brass knocker on the door must, she imagined, have happy people inside it ; at any rate, it furnished opportunities for happiness, which all respectable people would gladly take advantage of, if they could afford them.

People who live in Shoreditch, or St. George's-in-the-East, are apt to be confounded with their poorer neighbours by the uninitiated, although the initiated know that there is a greater distance between a dressmaker and a charwoman than between a countess and the wife of a successful merchant. It is a royal failing to see no difference between a nobleman and a lackey ; so the uninitiated must be pardoned for their ignorance in confounding together shop-keepers, artizans, labourers, and casuals. The initiated are aware how wide is the step which separates these people one from another, a wider step than that which the rich merchant's wife has to take when she enters society, because in society gold smelts "all sorts and conditions of men" together, while out of society there are no titles to barter for husbands and wives, no "positions" to buy men and women with.

"Who," pondered Polly (only she worded her thoughts in rather different language), "can doubt the respectability of a person occupying a little house in Hackney? A little house with venetian blinds in the windows, and a brass knocker on the door must hold respectable people, who pay their bills, go to chapel, and eat meat on Sunday."

Oh, the bliss of inhabiting a little house in Hackney!

Jos' thoughts lay in quite another direction. He was meditating whether he should light a pipe, and feasting his eyes on the green trees which he saw in the distance, trees with real foliage, not stunted trunks with make-believes for leaves, but green boughs reaching far up into the blue sky, making one think of the country.

"Let's sit down on the grass," he said to Polly, when they reached the Park.

"No," answered Polly, "I want to look at the people, and hear the music."

So they wandered on with the crowd, past the pond where the boats and ducks are, the stalls covered with sweets and buns, the stands holding ginger-beer and lemonade, to the band.

Victoria Park is one of the few places in which the public can indulge its Sunday taste for music. The men in high hats who there play stringed instruments, probably confer more pleasure than do the greatest opera-singers, for their audience is less critical and more appreciative than ladies and gentlemen who can afford guineas for stalls and boxes. Tired mothers luxuriate there under the trees, listen to simple tunes, and doze over their babies ; boys and girls play about ; men enjoy pipes and gossip. Young men and maidens, old men and women, dream there of the future and of the past. No West End face is to be seen there, no well-dressed man or woman ; only workers bent on enjoying their one day of relaxation, on making the most of the few hours they can call their own during the week.

Polly had never been to the Park before, and she was not quite sure that the band ought to be playing secular music on a Sunday afternoon. She determined to consult her class-leader about it, and never to come again if he said that she did wrong in coming.

But being there, and feeling that her presence made no difference,—that is to say, if she went away the band would go on playing as usual,—she determined to let Jos enjoy himself, and to say nothing to him about her qualms of conscience.

" What time is it ? " she asked presently.

Jos put his hand in his pocket.

He drew his hand back, and stared stupidly at Polly.

" What time is it ? " the girl repeated.

" I've lost my watch," Jos said hesitatingly.

" Lost it ? "

" Well, I mean, I haven't got it," Jos continued, "and I don't know when I'll see it again."

" Jos," exclaimed Polly, " you've pawned it ! "

" What if I have ? " asked Jos, with a quick look at his sweetheart.

" Nothing," said Polly, casting her eyes down, and moving on. " Let's see what that crowd's there for under those trees. There's a gentleman preaching."

They reached the trees, and found a thick mass composed of men and women tightly wedged together, revolving round some men who were arguing and lecturing on all sorts of subjects connected with politics and religion.

" My friends," said a lecturer, a black man with a flower in his button-hole, and his hat at the back of his head, " I have come here to teach you about the evolution of God. Without a knowledge of this great scientific truth nothing can be understood. I have evolved ; you have evolved ; *God* has evolved."

" Fellow-workmen," shouted a Socialist, "how long will you put up with this class oppression ? Don't you know that the men who rule over you are but a handful, and nothing to be afraid of ? If you are men, rise up ! Claim your rights ! Don't cower under the scowl of landlords and capitalists, turncoats like Chamberlain, tyrants like Salisbury ! Show yourselves men ! "

" Take my word for it, as one born and bred

in the country, the land isn't worth the having," said a Conservative working-man. "My father would have jumped out of his skin to get land at the price I can get it, and I would not have it for the giving. Go into the country and see for yourselves. Don't listen to people in towns, men that don't know turnips from carrots, young cabbage from chickweed."

"I've come here to learn," said a mild-eyed individual to a fiery little preacher, "and I don't understand. You say God *must* be just, yet He *may* be merciful. How do you reconcile these things? You speak of Free-will, and believe in Predestination. Perhaps you will explain how men can get to heaven who are destined to go to hell."

"God is all a trick of conscience," shouted a Free-thinker; "I take the Bible literally. I don't care for your celestial spectacles. If my conscience tells me to do a thing, and I do it, there's no God there, only conscience."

"Let's get away from these dreadful people," said Polly; "their talk's downright wicked. Come away, Jos."

"Well, I rather like to hear them talking," Jos answered. "I don't care for the black chap with his Latin and Greek, but I don't mind the fellow with the flag. Don't you remember him, Polly,—the one in the crowd yesterday who said the Queen ought to give a dinner or something down here, not to let people spend such a lot of money on her ? "

" I've always heard as chapel folks are much stricter than church folks," Polly answered. "You can stay if you like, I sha'n't."

" I've got his address," said Jos.

" You don't mean to visit him ? "

" Perhaps I do, perhaps I don't."

" There'll be no blessing on you if you mix with such folks," Polly told him. " Hark ! they're singing hymns over there. Let's hear them."

Jos looked curiously at the pretty Methodist. But her eyes were cast down, so she did not see him looking. He turned away with a smile, and followed her to a group of women and children gathered about a harmonium. As they went, he noticed men lying on the grass, some awake, some asleep, all more or less ragged ; many of them looked hopeless, careless of what went on around them, glad to lie like logs on the ground. They formed an ugly contrast to the people singing hymns, the men and women under the trees listening to speeches, and the crowd near the band. Jos did not like to look at them. Something seemed to tell him they had fallen out of the ranks, and that the great army was marching on without taking any notice of them, without asking why they had fallen out, and where they were going to.

"Jesus of Nazareth passeth by," sang Polly.

"He's been a long while passing," thought Jos. "Anyhow, people have got accustomed, and don't take much notice."

"What time is it?" inquired Polly.

"I've got no watch," answered Jos, with some bitterness.

"Oh! I forgot. Well, I think I'd better go home now. I mustn't be late for chapel."

"Don't be silly!" she told her lover a little later, when he tried to kiss her. But she let him do it, although she thought fit to remonstrate. They strolled slowly towards the Park entrance, and, if they did not talk much, Jos managed to do a good deal of silent love-making. He would have liked to spend the evening in the Park, but Polly was obdurate. The red tram would, she said be waiting at the corner, so they must be quick. She was a little offended with Jos. He had not offered her any tea, only a bottle of ginger-beer. Formerly he had been much more generous ; he had treated her to everything. She did not realise that his funds were low just then, nor did she suspect that they were fast dwindling to nothing. He was silent about his affairs, and she only broke his silence by inquiries as to whether he had found work, or was still doing nothing. In her thoughts Jos figured, as he affected her happiness. She prayed,

"O God, give Jos work, that he may marry me."

It did not enter her mind to pray, "O God, make Jos happy."

So they returned to Cannon Street on the top of a red tramcar, passing between festoons of paper flowers, flags, and banners which made Whitechapel look bright and gay, like a Continental city. Mottoes over shops welcomed the Queen Empress, showered good wishes on the Prince of Wales, and called down blessings on the whole Royal Family. The London hospital boasted of its many patients ; the big breweries were resplendent in red cloth and gold paper. The East End would not look so fine again for many a long year, perhaps never; for pageants are waning, and loyalty is dying, and kings and queens are fading away.

And all this because the people are tired of being "'ungry."

Jos accompanied Polly to her home, and hesitated when they reached the house. Perhaps he expected an invitation to tea, for he looked through the window at Mrs. Elwin, who was waiting for Polly. The little parlour appeared pleasant enough with a white cloth on the table, bread-and-butter, water-cress, and shrimps all ready for tea. Jos had had many a meal there. A few weeks before Mrs. Elwin would have made him welcome; but now she stroked the cat, and sat apparently unconscious of his presence.

"Good-bye," said Polly, holding out her hand, and casting her eyes downwards.

"Good-bye," said Jos.

She went into the house, he sauntered up the road again. He put his hat at the side of his head, and stuck his hands in his pockets. Presently he whistled the ghost of the Old Hundredth. He stopped whistling, and stared into a window at a picture of the Queen's last drawing-room. Then he moved on. At last he came to a small house in a small street, a dingy place with a dirty door and broken windows. He went in, and up a narrow, dark staircase to a bedroom. Here he opened a cupboard, and finding nothing inside, kicked the doors together. Half a loaf of bread was on the table ; he cut a bit of it with his pocket-knife. Sitting on the bed, he ate the crust which he had cut off the loaf, slowly, as though his teeth found it difficult to chew, and his tongue refused to swallow it. While eating he looked round the room, which was so small he could reach from wall to wall when he stood in the centre, and so dark he could not see the end opposite the window. Flies flew about, drowsy insects whose wings touched his face as he sat on the bed eating his supper. Not a book, not a picture was there, only bare walls, and a small table with one leg shorter than the other. The low bedstead had a straw mattress, no sheet, only a dirty blanket. Jos gazed in disgust at the wall opposite. Then he lighted his pipe, and walked to the window. He could see the roofs and chimneys of houses, also a lean black cat that lived among slates and bricks. Jos pushed his hat back, and put his elbows on the window-seat. He buried his chin in his hands, and stared gloomily at the chimneys. Church and chapel bells were ringing, and among the bells he seemed to hear the echo of bells he had known once, not long ago really, but at a time far back in his memory, a time as different from his present existence as light is from darkness. He watched the smoke rising from his pipe, curling up in the air, and as he watched he thought of the years those bells recalled, years spent in the country.

CHAPTER IV.

A DOCK-LABOURER.

"IT'S no good staying here all evening," he said at length. "I can't turn into those filthy blankets while it's daylight. I'll pay that man a visit."

He took a bit of paper out of his pocket, and looked at it. Then he shook the ashes from his pipe, put his hat straight, and went downstairs. When he reached the street he showed the bit of paper to a policeman, who happened to be standing near the house. The policeman read the address, and directed him towards Ratcliffe Highway.

"I wonder if we'll ever have any warm weather," Jos said to himself as he walked along, "I never remember a year like this with no spring in it."

Presently he began to think about the man whose address was written on the piece of paper, whose acquaintance he had made the previous afternoon, when he was standing on Mile End Waste, near the People's Palace. His attention had been attracted by a tall gaunt figure, with a thin eager face at the top of it; and when this strange-looking individual had begun to speak, he had listened open-mouthed, as became one fresh from the country.

"Why do you all stand here gaping?" the man had asked the crowd. "Don't you know the Queen's nothing but a selfish old woman, what doesn't care if we all starve, so long as she gets her own victuals? When did she put herself out for us?"

"Why do yer come yerself?" one of the crowd asked him. "Do yer think God Almighty would let the sun shine on her as He do, if she wasn't a good woman? Wherever she goes, and whatever she do, she has fine weather, bless her!"

The man gave a loud laugh. But before he could answer, Jos laid a hand on his arm, saying,—

"Don't, old chap. If you can't enjoy yourself, keep quiet."

"It's gospel truth," said the man, turning

round upon him. "You can't take nothing from it."

They began to argue, and before the Queen passed by, the man asked Jos to pay him a visit.

"You're not so green as you look," he told the young countryman, by way of a compliment. "As to these folks," he continued, waving his hand towards the crowd, "they're hopeless."

Jos reached the street he wanted, but looked in vain for the man's house. He walked up and down, looking. The number had, so a boy said, been altered. Only the previous afternoon two gentlemen had come to look for the very same house and the very same man. They had gone away disappointed.

It was a long, narrow street, with houses on either side of it. In the gutters was refuse, all sorts of garbage, that sent whiffs of stench on the cold evening breeze, to carry disease and death through the open windows of the over-crowded tenements. At the windows and on the doorsteps lounged women nursing children, and men in their shirt-sleeves. How so many people could have come together was a puzzle to Jos, whose limited acquaintance with the problems of life kept his mind in a chronic state of puzzling.

"P'raps," suggested a woman, "it's down farther end. I did hear as a number had been tacked on there. No. 2 used to be the corner shop, and when that was taken into t'other street, No. 2 was done away with."

Jos went to the end of the street as the woman suggested, stepping over children, and interrupting boys busy at tip-cat. There he found No. 2. It had no bell, no knocker; so he pushed the door open, went in, and groped his way up a dark, narrow staircase. Then he stood still; for he saw his acquaintance of the previous evening changed, metamorphosed.

The man was sitting by the fire, and on his knee lay a baby. He held the baby's head in the hollow of his right hand, with the other hand he tilted a feeding-bottle out of which the baby was sucking. His face was no longer grim and scornful. Its features had softened, every muscle had relaxed, and his thin lips were parted by a smile of tenderness. He did not see Jos for half a minute, not until a rosy-cheeked little woman said he was "wanted."

"Oh! it's you, is it?" he said then, looking up. "Come in, will you? The baby's ailing."

"Such a fine child as she was a fortnight ago," explained the mother; "her little arms and legs has gone to nothing."

Jos looked round the room. That one apartment was all the home these poor people could boast of. Its walls were black with smoke. Smuts had blackened Mr. Chamberlain's orchid, which was faithfully represented by a print on the wall. Smuts had settled on the nose of Mr. Bradlaugh, whose portrait was pinned above the fireplace. A bed covered with a patchwork counterpane filled one side of the place. The rest of the furniture consisted of boxes heaped one above another, a small table, and a wooden cradle. Household goods and chattels were piled on the boxes and scattered on the floor. The man's wife found it difficult to keep the place tidy, for he brought in a good deal of rubbish. Treasures *are* sometimes found in dust-heaps. In them he had discovered the torn works of more than one famous author, whose pages he had carefully cleaned and bound with brown paper. He had also bought some standard works in Petticoat Lane

Market off the trucks which West End book-
sellers supply with soiled volumes. Leaflets
received at meetings, and old newspapers picked
up in the streets, were littered about with the
books, making the room look as though some
costermonger of literature had upset his barrow
there. And in the midst of the confusion sat
the man nursing his child, while his rosy-
cheeked wife revolved like a satellite about his
chair.

That man had a very barren mental history.
He was one of the many people crushed out
by our present competitive system. He might
have been a statesman or a judge if he had
been born in more favourable surroundings.
He was no longer young. Time had grizzled
his hair and streaked his beard. His crude,
narrow ideas were fast crystallising. Years
had slipped by while he painfully and slowly
gathered crumbs of knowledge. His brain was
losing its power of gathering from fresh sources,
beginning to exercise itself upon the small
stores of knowledge stowed away in its cells.
Personal experiences had made him bitter. He
had only seen one side of life, and he did not
believe in what people call " happiness ; " un-

less, perhaps, the rich enjoyed it. Could they
be happy? Was it possible for them to enjoy
wealth knowing all that the poor are called
upon to suffer? Why not? Did not the angels
in heaven rejoice while the devils writhed in
torments? Men had created that heaven, that
hell, because they saw it daily before their eyes.
They had made a god like themselves. But
directly he looked at his child, the man was
metamorphosed. For its sake he tried to put
hope into his speeches, when he called upon his
fellow-workmen "to show themselves men."
He was hopeless himself, but the thought of
his child made him preach, if happily there
might be any good in preaching. Had he
been able to take his baby into Victoria Park,
to feel its little head in the hollow of his hand
when he stood on the Waste, he might perhaps
have risen to a pitch of enthusiasm, which would
have moved his hearers. Without that stimulus
he could only be bitter; and his bitter speeches
fell useless.

"What made you come to London?" he
asked, turning to Jos.

"Work got slack down where I was," Jos
said. "I was turned away, and as I had a bit

of money in the bank, what my mother had left me, I came to London."

" The worst place you could possibly come to."

" That's encouraging ! "

" Well, have you got any work yet ? "

" None."

" Have you heard of anything ? "

" Nothing."

" That's just what I expected. When you told me yesterday you were a carpenter, I said to myself, ' Whatever will the poor chap come to ? ' Why, hundreds of carpenters are out of work here—men who've been foremen, and earning their two and three pounds a week! You're nothing but a village artist ! "

Jos gave a gloomy smile.

" What do *you* do ? " he asked presently.

" I'm a dock-labourer."

" Where ? "

" At the Albert and Victoria—in the to-baccos. Have a smoke ? " the dock-labourer continued, drawing a small paper box from his pocket, and offering Jos a cigar. " I bring a few leaves home with me every evening,—not that I'm allowed to do it ; but I think it a sin to see good things wasted. Tobacco might grow in England from the way they leave it about the floor, and burn spoilt bales and sweepings. They let the men chew it, but if one is caught carrying it away with him, he is had up before the magistrate."

"Who made this?" asked Jos, taking the cigar from his mouth, and smacking his lips.

" I did. That's my trade. My father has one of the best tobacco businesses in Liverpool, and he turned me out when I became a Free-thinker.

" A nice sort of parent," Jos suggested.

" A Christian," said the dock-labourer. " If ever you take up with a Christian," he continued, lifting the baby from his knee, and looking at it, " I'll never forgive you. Don't cry, then. Only remember, Christians never hit straight; they don't know the meaning of being honest."

"One of them behaved very bad to his sister," whispered the rosy-cheeked woman to Jos; "he's never forgiven it. His sister did away with herself."

A pause followed, broken only by the whimpering of the baby. The father's stern face relaxed when he bent down to quiet it. Past memories disappeared, and he seemed only conscious of the little quivering bit of humanity on his knee, as he softly caressed the tiny head with one of his big fingers, and smoothed the downy hair on its forehead.

"Why is work so slack everywhere?" Jos asked the dock-labourer.

The man made no reply for a minute. Then he said,—

"I was arguing with an old neighbour yesterday, a Christian. I asked him if he believed in hell.

"'Of course I do,' he said.

"'Shall you go there?' I wanted to know.

"'No,' he said.

"'Shall I?'

"'I hope not.'

"'Then who will?'

"'Them furriners,' he said; 'they'll go to hell.'"

"Well, he's the rights on his side," exclaimed the rosy-cheeked little woman. "Why should they come here, I'd like to know? London ain't what it used to be; it's just like a foreign city. The food ain't English; the talk ain't

English. Why should all them foreigners come
here to take food out of our mouths, and live
on victuals we wouldn't give to pigs?"

"We've no right to wish them away, according to our doctrines," said her husband, getting
up, and laying the sleeping baby carefully in
the wooden cradle. "And I'm sure when
I see what the poor things will put up with,
I haven't the heart to wish them in a worse
place than London, bad as they make it for us
English."

He put on his hat, and invited Jos to go with
him out on the Waste. A keen blast slammed
the door after them, a cutting wind blew round
the corner as they left No. 2, and proceeded
to the place where working-men hold their
Sunday evening meetings.

"Did it ever strike you how nice it would
be to have a wife that understood things?"
asked the dock-labourer. "I mean a woman
like what educated men marry? I've courted
lots of girls in my time, and when I went
courting, we walked along, my girl and me,
without speaking. I gave her a kiss sometimes, but I kept my thoughts to myself; I
didn't trouble her with what I was thinking.

It's the same with my wife. She's a rare one with her tongue about some things, but she only knows how to mind the house and look after the baby. What's more, she looks on me as a sort of lunatic."

Jos remembered how silent he was with Polly, that he did not say much to her, or expect her to say much to him. This dock-labourer was a puzzle to Jos. He talked like a book, yet he could not have had much more learning than Jos himself. Jos supposed that his cleverness came natural to him, because he was a Londoner, for Londoners have (so people say) more ideas than have country bumpkins.

It was quite dark by the time they reached the Waste, and only a few gas-lamps threw their dim light upon the masses of men there gathered together.

" I won't speak to-night," said the dock-labourer, " there's some one at it already."

They drew nearer to listen.

" I'd like to know if there are sadder sights anywhere than those we now see around us ?" a young man was saying ; " I mean the homes of honest working men who have nothing to do, skilled workmen whose trades are itching

5

at their fingers' ends, who spend their days tramping about looking for work, and come home at night with empty pockets to hungry wives and children? I need draw no picture of these things. You not only see them, but *feel* them. You know what it is to have wives fainting for want of food, and children crying for crusts you cannot give them. In London alone thousands of men are out of work, and throughout the United Kingdom a million men are seeking employment. Who will help you? Mr. Chamberlain? He has dropped his ransom theory like a red-hot coal, and joined what he is pleased to call the Gentlemen of England.

"Mr. Bradlaugh? He is looking out for a seat in the next Liberal Government. Public Opinion? It takes long to form, for the public is wilfully ignorant. Custom is the god people worship, and until enough men and women have sacrificed themselves on the altar of established habits, Public Opinion will not be formed in favour of equality and justice. The clergy? They preach about the carpenter's Son to congregations who would scorn to invite Jesus of Nazareth to their grand parties, who put Him to an open shame by their inconsistent conduct. They say He is coming again. When He comes, they will not recognise Him; and He perhaps will not recognise them. You must help yourselves. You must join us in the class war which Socialists are now waging against your oppressors. Once united, no one can withstand you; you will be your own masters. You know our doctrines, help us to spread them. Speak to others of the co-operation which we propose to substitute for the present hateful competitive system. Tell them of the good time in store for themselves and their children. You are in the throes of a revolution. You are suffering that your class may be delivered. Hasten the time of delivery by your own efforts; do not let your sufferings prove useless.

" Let it be, if possible, a peaceable revolution. Use the weapons, propaganda and votes, rather than swords and bullets. Because you are hungry, do not grow hopeless. Everything is possible if once you are united. Remember it is not England alone, but America and the whole of Europe that join us in this great movement. Competition has had its day; it *must* give place to co-operation, because co-operation is the next step in the evolution of society ; it has a scientific basis. Individualists may try to stop it, but it cannot be stopped. The organisation of labour and the brotherhood of men are scientific truths which *must* be demonstrated. Join then in the struggle. Be Socialists."

CHAPTER V.

THE following day Polly had a talk with her class-leader. She laid her sewing aside, picked the shreds of cotton off the carpet, stuck the pins in the pincushion, and put on her hat and jacket. The room she worked in was like herself in appearance, neat and modest. It had a small bed in one corner, a chest of drawers facing the window, a washing-stand, and two chairs against the walls. A narrow looking-glass was fastened above the fireplace, and beneath this, on the mantel-piece, were china ornaments, representing shepherds and shepherdesses, a little Samuel saying his prayers, and a little girl reading the Bible. The pictures on the walls were works of art which Polly herself had executed. One picture showed a thrush with real feather plumage, red worsted beak, black beads for eyes, and yellow legs worked in worsted. It stood amongst dried moss and grass, drinking out of a brook, the silk waters of which were shaded blue, green, and violet. Polly had made another picture, which was even more ingenious than the thrush —namely, a worsted cottage, which formed the frontispiece of a landscape. Above the cottage shone the sun, and behind it hid the moon. The lesser light only showed a little bit of its circumference, and was probably put there to hint that night was coming, although the sun blazed full on a young man and a young woman, who stood hand in hand before the cottage, kissing.

Polly took a Wesleyan hymn-book off the chest of drawers, and then tripped downstairs, heedless of Mary Anne, who was rubbing her eyes after a scolding from Mrs. Elwin. She shut the front door, and went towards the chapel in which the day before she had attended " divine worship."

It was evening. Men had left their work, and stood about public-houses. Children crowded the pavements. Here and there a hurdy-gurdy kept the people dancing, boys with boys, girls with girls, even mothers nursing babies. Polly had nothing in common with the young women, whose untidy clothes and hair made her shudder ; and they sometimes threw an envious look at the pretty Methodist, who, with eyes on the ground, in neat dress and hat, went on her way, a way altogether unknown to fringes and draggled feathers. So she passed through some of the worst streets our metropolis can boast of, full of degraded human beings, filthy over-crowded houses, and shops that sell adulterated grocery, putrid meat, watered milk, and second-hand clothing. She reached the Wesleyan chapel, and went into a building beside it, a school used for children in the daytime, and Methodist classes in the evening.

Here she found her class-leader by himself, waiting for his class, of which Polly was the only member who never failed in attendance. He sat in a chair, looking gravely before him, with a little book in his hand, Mr. Augustus Hyde's word to objectors, waverers, and members. He had been considering why his class was so irregular, wondering if he had let escape any opportunity of impressing upon its members the duty of coming to him once a week for spiritual advice and assistance.

His appearance was well suited to his religious calling. He had a long face, a broad high forehead, and large full lips ; the hair on his head was thin, and rather long in the nape of his neck ; the hairs of his moustache might have been counted. He was seen to perfection when singing a hymn, for then he raised his eyes to the ceiling, moved his head backwards and forwards with the music, and looked every inch of him "a class-leader." His long frock-coat had a Methodist cut ; it was kept in a cupboard, and only used for Sunday wear, and during classes. Methodists have not as yet adopted that abomination of desolation,—a velveteen jacket,—although no doubt, they will some day ; they wear what used formerly to be wedding garments, namely, frock-coats, which are certainly less effeminate then velveteen jackets.

For two years Polly Elwin had had the benefit of this young man's instructions, and her mother said that it was wonderful to witness the growth in grace which his fostering care had produced in the pretty Methodist. Mrs. Elwin knew no terms high enough in which to express admiration and respect for

this godly youth. She invited him constantly
to tea on Sunday, and would have asked him
to dinner, had it not been for Uncle Cohen.
The Jew sparred with all Methodists except
Polly and his hostess. Moreover, he sometimes hinted that it was no unpleasant thing
to be a class-leader. He said that he would
willingly act shepherd himself, supposing that
Polly were the ewe lamb who needed his spiritual advice and assistance.

Mrs. Elwin shook her head over him, and
quoted Mary at the feet of Jesus in justifica-
tion of Wesleyan class arrangements. She
declared that it was well for a young man and
young woman sometimes to come together as
brother and sister, especially for a girl like
Polly, whose father was dead and buried, who
had but one parent.

"William Ford's a godly young man," she
said, "what will make a good husband to a
godly young woman. It isn't likely as Polly 'll
have the luck to marry her class-leader."

"Now I sometimes think," said the Jew,
"as William Ford's sweet on Polly. He's a
queer way of looking at her, a way of looking
what I can't understand, lest it's lovemaking."

"To hear you talk," scoffed Mrs. Elwin, "one would think you were a young man yourself, and jealous."

"What is a class meeting?"

"It is a meeting for the guidance and help of those who 'desire to flee from the wrath to come.' It is an inner circle of Christian communion, in which members of the Church meet together once a week to speak of their religious experience, and to receive advice from one called their class-leader on matters touching their spiritual welfare and opportunities of doing good."

"What is a class-leader?"

"A Methodist class-leader is generally an individual of mature Christian experience, sober, just, and temperate in all things. He gathers around him his little flock week by week, endeavours to ascertain, as far as possible, the spiritual state of each, and then imparts such advice as an enlightened judgment, guided by the Holy Spirit, may suggest."

So says Mr. Augustus Hyde in the little blue-book which William Ford had beside him, a book much akin with the one he was reading when Polly pushed open the door, and came into the schoolroom that evening.

" It's very warm," he said, greeting her.

" Yes," said Polly, " it's like summer."

A pause followed, during which Polly found a place in her Wesleyan hymn-book.

" It don't look as if any one but you were coming to-night," the leader said presently, drawing his chair a little nearer to Polly.

" I don't think it do," answered the pretty Methodist.

Neither spoke again for two or three minutes. Then Polly said,

" I was at Victoria Park yesterday afternoon. I don't know if I did right to go there of a Sabbath. They play tunes that ain't hymn-tunes, and talk about all sorts of things. I saw some children dancing."

" What made you go there?" inquired the leader.

" Jos wanted to see it."

" Who's Jos?"

" The man I'm going to marry."

One of the hairs on the leader's upper lip trembled. He closed Mr. Augustus Hyde's little book, glanced at Polly, and said,

" I didn't know you were going to be married."

"Oh! we can't marry yet," Polly told him. " Jos has no work. He's church."

" Church, is he ? "

" Yes."

" Church folks ain't half as strict as chapel people."

" That's what I said to Jos yesterday. He's been brought up by church people. His mother was a church lady."

"Where did you meet him ? "

" He came to our house as a lodger, up from the country. Now he's gone to another lodging, because he's out of work, and can't pay much. Leastways that's what he tells us. And mother," Polly hesitated, " mother says he oughtn't to come courting."

The leader drew his chair still closer to Polly.

" I don't like mother being vexed," the girl continued ; " she won't let Jos come inside the house. I wish he'd get work. Mother says young men can always find plenty to do if they ain't lazy."

" What's his trade ? "

" He's a carpenter."

" That's a good business."

" He says hundreds of carpenters are out of
work now, men who've been foremen. He
thinks Jews and foreigners do jobs so cheap he
hasn't a chance. Country carpenters, he says,
don't understand business like London men;
they ain't accustomed to such big roofs, and
window casings ain't what he's made down in
the country."

" Why did he come to London ? "

" Work got slack where he was, and he was
turned away."

" I don't believe that," said the leader,
slowly. " It isn't a likely story. I've been in
the Mint ever since I was a boy. If I was
turned away, it would be for some good reason,
I shouldn't be turned away for nothing."

" That's what mother says," remarked Polly.
" Mother says, ' See William Ford ; he's got
work, he's not been turned away.' Mother
thinks Jos was lazy or something. She hasn't
got a good word for him."

Before the leader could answer, the door
opened, and another member of his class
appeared on the threshold. All he had time to
say was,

" You should not go against your mother,"

and, "if I were you I wouldn't go to Victoria Park any more on the Sabbath."

"Let us pray," he continued, when the unpunctual member had joined Polly. He knelt down, folded his hands, and lifted his eyes upwards.

"O Lord!" he read out of a little book, "Who in Thy great mercy hast caused to be instituted a means of grace like the Methodist class meeting, and hast directed Thine unworthy servant to have her name enrolled as a member of that Society; listen while Thine unworthy servant confesses with shame how poorly she deserves such a privilege, and how little use she makes of the spiritual instruction she may receive there. Help Thy unfaithful servant from this day forward to observe a better course of conduct, and cherish a greater respect for her class-leader."

After this prayer had been said, the class continued in the usual form of Methodist classes; and when the trio separated, Polly went home thinking,

"What a godly young man is my class-leader!"

CHAPTER VI.

JOS LOOKS FOR WORK.

THAT very same Monday Jos woke up early in the morning, just as the air was at its freshest, and the sparrows were beginning to twitter outside his window. He got out of bed, and wondered at first what was the matter, for the furniture in the room seemed dancing round him, and in his head was a buzzing noise, as though half-a-dozen kettles were singing there together. Outside the window all looked blue, inside the room a red hue was on everything. He fell back on the bed.

Then cold drops of perspiration came on his forehead, and he shivered; for an icy chill crept from his feet upwards, a cold band seemed to tighten round his waist, and his head felt like lead on the pillow.

"I'll try again," he said.

He got up, and this time he stood firm on

his feet. He was able to walk towards the window, where he drank a glass of water, and the morning air sent the blood back from his head to circulate through his chilly members. His brain became once more capable of thinking.

"I guess I know what's up with me," he said. "I'm hungry."

He remembered that he had eaten nothing but dry bread the previous day, and that for some time before he had not had a dinner. A herring in an eating-house, a halfpenny cup of tea or coffee at Lockhart's, had for the last week been his daily fare, together with a "customer," which he kept in his cupboard, and washed down with draughts of water.

"I'll not take any more of that," he said, looking at the bottle out of which he had just been drinking, at the bottom of which lay a thick coating of stuff like verdigris ; "it tastes as if a dozen cats had been drowned in it."

Afterwards he took up the remains of the "customer," which was hard as a brick.

"D— it !" he said, throwing the bread out of the window ; "I can't get my teeth through it."

Five minutes later he left the house, and

went across the Whitechapel Road, down
Cambridge Street, to a place where the *Daily
Chronicle* is pasted on some old palings.

A crowd of men stood there, fighting for
room, ramming their heads into one another,
climbing on one another's shoulders, or creeping
in between one another's legs, to read the
advertisements. This scramble took place in
silence, except when a man spelt out a word
or sentence in gutteral accents, very unlike
those in which he had learnt to read at school.
Jos could not get to the palings for nearly ten
minutes, but he slowly wedged his way in by
patient pushing, and stood still, with heads
bumping against his shoulders, elbows jostling
him on all sides, and feet stamping on his toes.
Why had he come there ?

He might have known that coming there
was useless.

So he said to himself, as he ran his eye down
the advertisements, and did not find any one of
his trade wanted, although carpenters, joiners,
and cabinet-makers advertised themselves as
willing to do *any* work at *any* rate of payment.
A gloomy smile came over his face as he recol-
lected the advertisement which he had himself

6

inserted, when he had had money to throw away, when he first came up from the country.

"Carpenter, punctual, industrious, sober, with excellent character, well supplied with tools, seeks engagement." Of course he had received no answer to this, any more than he had received answers to the various letters which he had sent on seeing advertisements.

Oh yes ; he had had one once. It had said, "Messrs. Gilby and Smith regret to inform Mr. Joseph Coney that he is not wanted."

As he moved away from the palings the crowd grew less. Some of the men went home again, others lounged off to lie on benches about squares, and on the grass in parks. A few lolled into public-houses, there to spend their last penny, and to concoct at the bar some plan of doing something, when a glass of gin had changed grim realities into possibilities of better things, had thrown a veil over dramas at home, such as hungry wives and starving children, who could not go out of doors because their rags of clothes were in pawn-shops.

Jos walked as fast as he could to a tall building which some company was running up, in

order to house the poor at a lower rate of payment than in ordinary lodging-houses, by
crowding them closer together.

("Such jerry work," workmen were wont to
say with smiles of contempt, as they watched
the walls springing up, windows appearing as if
by magic, and all the cheapest inventions being
brought to fill in this artizans' dwelling.)

It was only half-past five o'clock, but about
the jerry building hung a crowd of respectable-
looking men, with baskets of tools in their
hands, and that look on their faces which says
" I know my business." Some nodded to Jos,
but most gave him a sullen glance as he came
down the street, like that which a dog with a
bone throws at another dog less lucky than
itself. The whole conversation was about
work. Had this man seen in the *Builder* that
such a place was going to be built ? Had
that man heard that a new bridge was completed ? Who were the contractors for the
Jubilee affair ? Who would give jobs at
Westminster Abbey ?

Presently the foreman appeared, and the men
divided to let him pass into the jerry building.
A grim silence fell everywhere, for on him

depended their chance of carrying home a little money that evening.

He came slowly out again. He called on half-a-dozen men, and told the rest that they were not wanted. Two hundred men stood there, and only six were required—six skilled hands, who a few years before had commanded twice the money they could earn on that jerry building.

Jos knew that he had no chance there. He was, as the dock-labourer had told him, nothing but a village artist.

He could not hoist a roof, or build a staircase well enough to satisfy a London foreman; but he went there because he was afraid of losing a chance, and he might as well be there as anywhere else. He must be doing something.

As he turned away he remembered that a carpenter named Reeson lived close by, a man who had given him a kind word one day, when he was hanging about a shop in Holborn, with hundreds of other applicants, for a place which had been advertised as vacant. He thought that he would look the man up, and ask if anything anywhere gave hope of employment for a village artist.

So he went to a huge ungainly-looking block that stretched halfway down the street, and ran up so high that he could not see the roof, only the chimneys of it.

He passed through some iron gates into a long asphalte court. " What's that big building opposite?" he asked a small boy who was washing himself in a tub, and drying his face with a dirty pocket-handkerchief.

"Sure, and it's the Mint," replied the lad, grinning. " What else should it be, thin?"

"That's where William Ford works," thought Jos. And a spasm of jealousy shot across him, for, although he had never seen the leader, Polly had quoted the godly young man as one who had regular employment, and Mrs. Elwin had spoken of Polly's spiritual adviser with reverence in Jos's presence, as though she thought that a man who handled so much money must have some of it lining his pockets.

" I'm too soon to see Reeson," thought Jos.

But he remembered that the carpenter had said, " Come very early or very late, if you want to find me in ; " so he went up a narrow dark staircase, to a small green door, and knocked.

The door was opened by a tall thin woman, whose face had that expression of chastened suffering which only comes after long years of misery, during which hopes have been so invariably disappointed, that the mind has recoiled on itself, and settled down into hopelessness.

She was a woman "past crying;" for Nature cannot make tears for ever; and this poor thing had cried so much that she had exhausted all the tears Nature could give her.

"Is Mr. Reeson in?" Jos asked, glancing into the room, which had a bundle of rags in one corner, and a three-legged chair by the window.

"No. He has started," the woman said.

"Where has he gone to?"

"To look for a job."

"Hasn't he had work lately?"

"He can't have had, or he'd have brought something home with him," the woman answered. "I never ask no questions. It only angers him if I do. He'd a good temper when we married, but now his temper's got cantankerous. Come in, won't you? What message shall I give him?"

Jos walked into the room, and there he saw

two large cards, ornamented with strange devices, hanging on the walls.

" That," said the woman, pointing to the card above the empty fireplace, " is the Ancient Order of Druids ; t'other is the Supreme Order of Buffaloes."

"What do you mean ? " asked Jos, staring at her.

" The Ancient Order of Druids has buried our six children," said the woman solemnly, "and it'll bury me when I die. The Supreme Order of Buffaloes will bury my husband, and give him a pound a week when he's so ill, the doctor says maybe he's dying."

" That's buried six kids ? " said Jos, taking his eyes off the woman, and fixing them on the card above the fireplace.

" Yes. They're tidy funerals. The last one had a coffin fit to bury the Queen in."

At that minute the door was opened, and Reeson came in. He took no notice of Jos, but threw his tools on the ground, and flung himself upon the three-legged chair by the window.

"What is it then ? " asked his wife.

Reeson made no answer ; he buried his head

in his hands, and great sobs shook his whole body.

"You'd best go away," said his wife to Jos. "I suppose he's made up his mind to it. We'll have to go to the workhouse. We owe a month's rent, and if he can't get a job they won't let us bide here any longer. We've had to borrow money for them," she continued, pointing to the Supreme Order of Buffaloes, and the Ancient Order of Druids, "but we can't go on a-borrowing. To think this is what we've come to! And he was a master-carpenter when we married!"

"If master-carpenters can't get work, whatever will become of village artists?" wondered Jos.

He left the block, and walked towards Lockhart's shop, which is close to the Mint. As he went he saw men sitting on the stones by the post-office, rough fellows with hungry faces and famished eyes. It was nearly time for them to begin hanging about the docks, to commence looking out for a job, at the only place where a man can get work without having a character. For at the docks a baronet is found cheek by jowl with a loafer

from Whitechapel, a clergyman works beside
an escaped convict. The company there is
more mixed than anywhere else in London, so
whoever sinks into it can never rise up again,
is socially branded.

"Shall I come to *that?*" wondered Jos, as
he swallowed his halfpenny cup of coffee, and
ate a stale bun. "Not if I can help it. But
what *shall* I come to?"

Then he began the weary tramp which he
had accomplished every day lately. He went
to all the buildings on which he thought a
carpenter could possibly be wanted, he waited
outside shops, he walked miles and miles, hour
after hour, resting sometimes for a few minutes,
then tramping on again. Time passed, and he
found himself in the fashionable part of London,
in Hyde Park. Weary and footsore, he sank
down on a seat by the gate through which
grand ladies drive in still grander carriages,
smart gentlemen ride on still smarter horses;
and sitting there he realised that not one of
these lords and ladies (so he called them)
knew what it was to be hungry, had felt the
sting of being "out of work," the pang of
feeling "I am not wanted."

" I don't envy them nothing," he said to himself, "but they needn't look so scornful-like. They're but flesh and blood, though they be lords and ladies. They all look here as they did down Mile End Waste way last Saturday, as though God Almighty hadn't made we, nothing but lords and ladies." He went on again, on, on, on ; getting each hour fainter, yet not daring to buy food until he reached home. His money was fast slipping through his fingers, and he had not earned a single penny since he set foot in our great Babylon, which is so strangely divided into East and West, those who have, and those who have not.

"I don't want their fine things," thought Jos, as carriages rolled by, and horses trotted past. "I only want work. If God Almighty will give me a job, I'll ask no more of Him." At last he found himself back again in the slums, his own quarters.

He passed by the Tower, and went down to the river, where he took off his boots, and dipped his feet in the water. Tiny waves dashed against the stone walls, and broke on the steps where he sat. Vessels were moored here and there, little boats rocked up and down. He was alone, for it was growing dark and cold.

"I guess," said Jos, looking gloomily across the Thames, "I ain't wanted. There are too many of us poor folks, and not enough work for us to do."

CHAPTER VII.

POLLY AT A JUBILEE GATHERING.

DAYS went on. The Jubilee waxed towards its climax. The East End saw Jubilee herrings, Jubilee eggs, and Jubilee sugar-plums. Festivals and entertainments were organised even there in honour of Her most Gracious Majesty, who is called in Whitechapel the "old lady."

"We, too, must keep our Jubilee," said Mr. Meek, one Sunday morning, when he stood in the pulpit. "We will go to Reigate,—that is, all of us who can afford a five-shilling ticket."

So the following Saturday afternoon about fifty Methodists assembled on the platform of London Bridge Station, where Mr. Meek and Mr. Stry stood ready to receive them.

"All the babies with me," cried Mr. Meek, jovially; "I'm a family man. Jump in, jump in. Mothers and babies with me; young ladies with Mr. Stry; young men anywhere they can find places." Mr. Meek had been twice married.

"If I had not had *that* great sorrow," he sometimes said, pointing to his first wife's picture, "I could not have had *this* great joy," pointing to his second wife, a buxom young woman with a large progeny.

Mr. Stry was a bachelor. He had missed his vocation in life. He was meant to be a monk, not a Methodist. He would have done very well a century or so sooner, when the followers of Mr. Wesley were ducked in ponds, and stoned for their opinions, when women had convulsions, and men fell to the ground on hearing the warning voice of a Wesleyan minister; but in this age of loose opinions and Jubilee gatherings he was wasted. His lugubrious countenance only served to frighten small Methodists, whose mothers said, "I'll tell Mr. Stry if you bain't good directly;" who thought that he would drop them into the burning pit, which played such a large part in his Sunday School lessons, in his prayers and sermons.

The Methodists arrived safely at Reigate, and as they walked through the town people said,

"There goes another Jubilee party." Summer
had come at last, and was unusually fresh and
young, having sprung straight out of winter,
without its usual forerunner spring. Birds were
late in building, and flew busily about, picking
feathers and moss from the hedges. A breeze
ran along the grass, white clouds floated in the
blue sky. It was real Queen's weather, the
Methodists said, as they enjoyed their tea in
a field, under the shadow of some tall elm trees,
facing a long stretch of grass, with wooded hills
in the distance

After tea some of the Methodists played
cricket. Mr. Meek sat down among the mothers
and babies ; Mr. Stry strolled away to enjoy
a silent colloquy with Mr. Wesley ; every one
was free to enjoy himself, or herself, according
to his, or her, good pleasure. So it came to
pass that Polly Elwin found herself gathering
dog-roses in an adjacent field, not alone, but
with that godly young man, William Ford, who
thought it right to improve the occasion by an
out-door lesson.

"They make one think of women in the
Bible," he remarked, while he stuck some wild
roses in his buttonhole, and looked sentiment-

ally at Polly, "women that have the ornament of a meek and quiet spirit."

Polly said " Yes."

" This one's like you," he continued, cutting a small pink-and-white bud with his huge pocket-knife, and giving it to Polly ; " it's neat and modest."

Polly blushed.

' How's that man ? " he asked presently.

"What man ? "

" That man you're going to marry.   Has he got work yet ? "

Polly shook her head.

" What's he like ? "

" I don't know," answered Polly.   " I've never thought."

" Is he like me ? "

" Oh no ! "

"Who's he like then ? "

" No one as ever I've come across," the girl replied slowly, looking away to the hills, and thinking of Jos.   " He's like himself."

" I've turned over in my mind all you told me last class," the leader said after a pause, during which Polly picked roses, and he had time to frame a sentence.   " I've given it a deal of prayer and thought. I'm afraid a man who'd go to Victoria Park pleasure-making on the Sabbath, can't be converted. Are you sure he's saved, Miss Elwin?"

Polly stopped picking roses, looked at the leader, and said, "He's church."

"The Bible tells us not to be unequally yoked," continued the leader. "I don't mean to say that church folks can't get saved, if they go the right way to work, but I DO say as folks should be careful who they marry."

Polly was silent.

"Has he spoken to you about his soul?" inquired the godly youth.

"No," replied Polly. "He's mostly quiet, is Jos; he don't talk much."

"It's a solemn thing to be married," the leader remarked, "a thing not to be done in a hurry. I hope you pray for the light of God on what you're doing, Miss Elwin. Maybe God is saving you from trouble by not letting that man get work." Polly was very much impressed by the leader's last sentence; she had been brought up on such illogical stuff. She was accustomed to see Providence where He was wanted, to ignore Him when His presence proved inconvenient.

" Let's rest a bit," the leader suggested. They sat down under a hedge, and watched the sun set, a sun that rises on the just and the unjust, on Turks, infidels, and heretics, as well as Wesleyan-Methodists.

Polly took off her hat, and smoothed the soft fair hair on her forehead. The leader lay at her feet, and threw a covert glance of admiration when she dropped the roses on her knee, and proceeded to pick them up again. Then he looked towards the setting sun, wrapt in meditation.

Before the girl's eyes a picture rose up. She saw herself being married in the Wesleyan chapel. Mr. Meek held a wedding-ring. Mr. Stry read the marriage-service. The bridegroom was not Jos, but the class-leader. The whole congregation looked on, some admiring, some envying, all possessed with the idea that the bride was about to have "a position." For the class-leader was well known to the little circle Polly lived in. They knew him as a godly young man, who worked in the Mint, who had a settled income.

No one in Polly's circle knew Jos. When he first came to her mother's house, a smart

7

young carpenter, with *two boxes*, Polly talked about him to her intimate friends. After her engagement she hinted that they meant to live in Hackney, in a little house, to which the butcher would pay constant visits. All that Polly s circle could hear *now* about Jos was, " He's out of work." So Polly kept a discreet silence, and her mother ignored the engagement. Mrs. Elwin had never liked Jos ; and had only given her consent to the marriage with sundry shakes of the head, and hints that it was not the sort of match the late-lamented Mr. Elwin would have liked for his daughter. Lately (as Polly said) she had not a good word to say for the young carpenter ; she could not understand how a man in his position "had the face to come courting."

The sun sank down behind the wooded hills, not a ray of purple was left on the horizon. A dull grey covered the sky. The birds ceased twittering, and settled themselves for the night. A cold wind took the place of the breeze ; Polly rose up, and William Ford slowly followed her example.

" We'd best see what the others are doing," said Polly.

So they went back to the field in which they had had tea, and there they found all the Methodists gathered together (except Mr. Stry who was still soliloquizing with Mr. Wesley) under the elm trees.

"You're just in time," cried Mr. Meek. "We're going to fire a volley of kisses!"

By some strange coincidence when the volley took place, William Ford found himself standing beside the pretty Methodist. Stranger still,— as his thick lips touched Polly's cheek, the girl felt a shudder run through her ; she longed to wipe the kiss away with her pocket-handker-chief.

"One volley more in honour of Queen Victoria!" cried Mr. Meek.

And again the thick lips touched Polly's pink-and-white cheek. Why was it that the leader's thick lips sent a shudder through the pretty Methodist? Half an hour before she had pictured herself as his wife ; now, strange to say, she shrank away from him, and centred her thoughts upon Jos. She took refuge among the mothers and babies, and on the way home she asked for a seat in Mr. Meek's carriage. Directly the train left the station she

rubbed her cheek with her pocket-handkerchief.
As the stars came out she looked through the
window, and wondered what Jos was about.
She had not seen him for nearly three weeks;
and she remembered that he had looked tired
the last time they went for a walk, that he had
seemed scarcely able to put one foot before the
other on the way home again.   " Jos, have you
got any work yet ? " had met with the usual
response ; and she had not thought of sym-
pathising with him.

She had almost felt that he was doing her an
injury by remaining "out of work ;" had almost
persuaded herself that her mother was right,
that Jos must be lazy.   But this evening, as
the stars came slowly out, and some one sang
" Wait till the clouds roll by " in the carriage,
she thought of her lover with all the tenderness
her little nature was capable of feeling, thought
of him apart from herself, thought of *his* happiness.   Where was he ?   What was he doing ?

" I do hope Uncle Cohen will be at the
station," she said to herself.   " William Ford
will take me home if he isn't."

Her mother had said, " I'll send Uncle Cohen
to meet you if I can't come myself ; " and as the

train reached London Bridge the girl strained her eyes to see the Jew; she longed for the sight of his long nose and crisp grey hair; and when she saw them she called out,

"Oh, Uncle Cohen, I was so afraid you wouldn't meet me!"

She scarcely waited to wish the Methodists good-bye. She laid her hand on the Jew's arm, and hurried him out of the station. Uncle Cohen had come there under protest. He expected that Polly would wish to walk home with some young man, not an old fogey like himself. Poor Uncle Cohen! He had put off marrying a little too long, as many a gay bachelor has done before him; and now he found that the days when he could have achieved domestic happiness had for ever vanished.

He loved Polly. He did not tell her so, of course, for she would only have laughed at him; but he loved her nevertheless, and hated every young man who set foot inside her mother's house. He was quite sure that the world did not hold a girl like her anywhere, not a girl so pretty, with such beautiful hair and teeth, and eyes—well, eyes like forget-me-nots.

Her father had been his greatest friend. He knew how to put up with all her mother's sayings and doings. He loved Polly more than any woman he had ever met, from the days when he began life as traveller for a large house of business, to the time when he settled down as hairdresser and dentist in Whitechapel. She was unlike the Jewesses who came to his shop, unlike anybody but herself; she was just his little Polly, the little girl who used to sit on his knee as a baby, and give him kisses.

"Uncle Cohen!" said Polly, resting her soft cheek on his arm, "I'm so unhappy, Uncle Cohen."

The Jew felt a lump rise up in his throat. It was a long, long time since she had been so affectionate.

"What's the matter, little woman?" he asked in a husky voice. "What is it?"

"I'm wondering where Jos is, what he's doing to-night."

CHAPTER VIII.

A DOSS-HOUSE.

JOS was on his way to a common lodging-house.

"You are sure to have a job for the Jubilee," people had told him.

So he had hoped and waited. But he had found five hundred carpenters hanging about Westminster Abbey, scores of whom had been foremen; and as to seats and scaffoldings, contractors for these had so many men on their lists there was no chance for a village artist.

That Saturday night while Polly was walking home with Uncle Cohen, Jos was on his way to a doss-house. He was afraid to stay out in the street, although he would have preferred to sleep there; for, if he did, a policeman might "run him in" (according to East End phraseology "a body-snatcher might grab him"). He would not go to a workhouse, for he had

fourpence in his pocket, enough to pay for one
more night of independence.   His last four-
pence !

He stopped under a lamp, and took the
following letter out of his pocket to read it :—

"·Rᴇᴠ. Sɪʀ,—I am extremely sorry that I have to
trouble you on my behalf, but, sir, I know you can
understand my position.   Well, sir, it is this, that
since I came to London I have found no work to do.
Well, sir, I have no money.   All the money my mother
put by is gone.   I have to tender my heartfelt thanks
to you for your great kindness to me, and especially to my
poor mother.   I hope and trust, sir, that this trouble
will soon pass away, but please, sir, send me some
money.   I will pay you back, sir, directly I get work.
Oh, sir, you cannot realise my feelings to have to ask
this through no fault of my own, it makes me sick with
misery.   If you will kindly grant me what I ask, I will
feel it a great obligation.

> "I remain,
>> " A poor man in adversity,
>>> "Jᴏꜱᴇᴘʜ Cᴏɴᴇʏ.

"Oh, sir, tell the men at home never to come to
London; there is no work for them here, nothing but
starving."

It was a letter to the clergyman in the village
he came from, the first begging letter he had
ever written in his life.   He put it back in his

pocket, although it had a stamp on the envelope.

"If I did wrong coming to London, it's not my fault," he thought. "There was no work to be had in the village, and London seemed the likeliest place to come to. Supposing I'd gone anywhere else, it would have been just as bad, I reckon. Work's slack everywhere; there's too many of us, and not enough work for us to do."

Walking along he thought of Polly Elwin. He felt glad she could not see him that evening, or know where he was going. For three months,—in fact, ever since he left her mother's home—his prospects had been growing more and more hopeless. To-morrow he must try to find work at the docks, for then he would be penniless.

Perhaps he ought to have told Polly all this. But the worse things looked, the more he seemed to cling to Polly Elwin. She was, as it were, the only link he had left with his past existence, the one straw that kept him from sinking.

Besides, he loved the pretty Methodist.

In what way?

It is commonly supposed that men of his class feel a sort of general spooniness, mixed with a good deal of animalism, for their sweethearts.

The truth was this. Jos had fallen in love with Polly the day he went to Mrs. Elwin's house as a lodger, the afternoon he had seen her bending over some sewing in the little sitting-room, looking so pretty and modest. Since that time she had formed a picture in his mind, a picture that somehow or other resembled his mother, that was in some vague way connected with things down in the country. He did not try to analyse his feelings ; but she was constantly before his eyes and in his thoughts. He remembered days they had spent together in the little sitting-room, before he became accustomed to the depravity and the filth of East End surroundings, when everything in London was new and strange to him, while he was still a country bumpkin. He recalled the evening on which he had asked her to be his wife. He said to himself, " *We'll* do this, and *we'll* do that, when I get work."

Give her up ? Such a thing never entered

his head. He meant to work at the docks until he had saved enough money to go on looking for an opening in his own business. He *must*, he thought, find something to do if he waited long enough. Meanwhile Polly need only know that he was "out of work." He would never tell her, and she would never guess, how hard up he had been, how near starving.

He reached the doss-house, and finding the door wide open, walked in. Then he stood still in a long, narrow room, looking. The lower part was almost dark, but at the further end a great fire blazed up the chimney. In the centre was a table with two lamps upon it. By the table sat a number of men, gambling.

"Man or homan?" asked a gruff voice.

"Homan."

"You deal then."

"'Ere goes my night's lodging."

"I'll stand you a bed, pal."

"Don't you stand 'im nothing."

Jos walked up to the last speaker and asked, "Where's the deputy?"

"I'm 'e. What do you want of me?"

"Can I have a bed?"

"Yes, if you can pay for it."

Jos silently handed the man his last four-pence.

"Come along," said the deputy. " I'll show you where to turn in. You can choose your sheets, and come back 'ere to enjoy yourself."

He lighted a dip candle, and led the way up a winding staircase.

"Mind your 'ead, stupid," he exclaimed, as Jos knocked his head against the slanting ceiling. " Why don't you look where you're going to ?"

Then he opened a door, and showed Jos a room full of small iron bedsteads, covered with grey blankets. They were arranged in two rows against the walls, and were so close together that it was almost impossible to move between them. In some men were already asleep, upon others men were undressing, or lying dressed outside the blankets.

" Can't I have a place to myself ? " asked Jos.

" Family rooms cost eightpence."

" Haven't you a fourpenny place ? "

"You're darned particler," grumbled the deputy, bringing the dip candle close to Jos' face, and examining him carefully. " I've 'ad your betters 'ere, young feller. This way then '

Jos followed him.

They went through rooms like the first, some full of men, some full of women, all equally crowded.

"We're under Mayhew's Act," the deputy once stopped to remark. "The police walk in and out as they like. We've clean sheets once a week, and a wash-house at the back. They're darned particler, are the police. They come after me and my missus like ferrets."

At last he opened a door leading into a small cupboard, and seated himself on the bed to contemplate Jos.

"You're down in your luck," he said gravely. "I'd a man in this room once what 'ad lost eighty 'orses with glanders, and 'e said to me when I brought 'im in, ' I can't sleep 'ere.' 'E did though for nearly a twelvemonth. Don't give in becos things look bad, young feller. The lower you sink, the nearer you come to the surface. I mean, many a man 'as to go to the bottom afore 'e comes to the top. I'll tell you *my* 'istory. The first night I slept in this 'ouse—long afore I come 'ere as deputy, mind you—I made the money for my night's lodging in a rum way. It was freezing 'ard, and I 'adn't a penny in my pocket. Well, I see'd some injin skins lying outside a greengrocer's shop, on a 'eap of rubbish. I picked 'em up. Says I to myself, I'll make injins on 'em. So I made some balls of frozzen snow, and licked the skins round 'em. I sold 'em for injins, and got my night's lodging."

" What's injins ? " asked Jos.

" Inions, of course."

" Onions ! "

" Well, call 'em what you like. I'm not particler. From that day my luck turned, I tell you ; I stayed on in this 'ouse, and now I'm deputy 'ere. Come along, I'll interdooce you to my missus."

They went downstairs again, and found the deputy's wife keeping order among the gamblers. He was a tall broad-shouldered man ; dressed in corduroy trousers, a cotton shirt, and bright red braces. She was a large, stout woman, of the same build as her husband. Standing there, with arms a-kimbo, feet wide apart, waist too large to be spanned by the arm of a Goliath, and short cropped hair, she might have been mistaken for her lord and master if she had not worn petticoats.

" Missus," the man said, clapping Jos on the

back, "'ere's a young feller what's down in
'is luck. I've given 'im the slip at the top of
the 'ouse cos he's darned particler, and don't
like to sleep with other folks."

The deputy's wife gave a loud laugh as Jos
moved away towards the fireplace.

Men and women stood there cooking their
supper ; emptying into tins and saucepans bits
of meat, bones, scraps of bread and cold potatoes
they had begged, stolen, or picked up during
the day. Hungry children held plates ready
for the savoury messes, and received blows and
kicks from their parents when they came too
near the fire, or interfered with the cooking
arrangements.

Crouching on the floor, gnawing a bone, was
a man closely resembling the "'ungry" man,
who about a month before had disturbed the
panegyric of the godly nation in the Wesleyan
chapel, who had wanted to see the corn and
wine of which Mr. Meek spoke so figuratively.

His face was soddened by drink. He had
swollen features, palsied hands, and trembling
feet. He had probably begun life in this Christian country as a homeless boy in the streets ;

and would most likely close his days in the casual ward of some workhouse. Then

> "Rattle his bones over the stones,
>   He's only a pauper, whom nobody owns!"

The lodgers threw him scraps, and laughed to see him tearing his food to pieces, devouring it like a dog, on the ground. Near him, resting her head against the wall, sat a young woman. She had a baby on her knees, a little thing, almost naked. Its chiselled limbs shone in the firelight. The mother's eyes were shut, and her heavy tears fell on it; so she did not see a shrivelled hag, with ragged clothes, and grey matted hair, watching her. Once the hag drew near to touch the baby's rounded knee with a claw-like finger. She drew back again, muttering. A minute later she joined the old man on the floor; and the lodgers made coarse jokes, while the two quarrelled together for crusts and potatoes.

Jos stood by the fire for a few minutes. Then he went to the door, and sat down there on a bench by a table. He buried his face on his arms, and tried to forget his surroundings.

Presently he heard a voice ask, "Aren't you 'ungry?"

He looked up, and saw a girl offering him a basin with a pewter spoon in it.

He shook his head.

The girl looked disappointed. " Eat it," she said.

She was scarcely more than a child, a little thing with large dark eyes, and black hair falling about her face.

" Ulloa, Squirrel ! '' cried the deputy, who was passing by, " the police is a-coming.''

The girl took no notice. She put the basin down before Jos.

" You'll never want for a meal if you're friends with the Squirrel,'' remarked the deputy. " I'd rather trust 'er than any one I know to steal me a dinner.''

He left the house, and the girl seated herself opposite the young carpenter, leaning her elbows on the table, resting her chin on her hands.

" Eat it,'' she repeated, fixing her great dark eyes on his face. " I'd breakfast.''

CHAPTER IX.

PENNILESS.

IT is difficult to realise the environment of another person, but still more difficult to know in what way that environment will modify his or her character. We almost always place ourselves in the position of the individual we are thinking about, and say, " I should do this or that, if those were my circumstances." The wisest of us often make this mistake ; so Joseph Coney, whose brains were of the same calibre as the brains of other young carpenters, who had not the intellectual capacity of an educated man, may be excused for expecting his sweetheart to act as he himself would have acted in her position. While walking along the Whitechapel Road the morning after his first night in the doss-house, he thought of Polly ; and he did not conceive that she was capable of changing, he did not suspect that she was drifting away from him.

"I'll find a job at the docks, and when I've money I'll go on looking for work in my own trade," he said to himself. "I *must* find something if I look long enough."

On leaving the doss-house a curious thing had happened to him. The Squirrel had darted up, and given him sixpence. She had pressed it into his hand, then run away, jumping from pavement to gutter, from gutter to pavement, until a turn of the street hid her altogether. Jos had not known what to do with the money, so he had put it into his waistcoat pocket. Walking along he contrasted the dark-eyed girl with the pretty Methodist ; and he seemed to know that Polly would not have guessed he was hungry, would never have suspected he was penniless.

It was late. He had not hurried out of bed that morning, he had taken his first lesson in laziness. Having made up his mind to work at the docks, he had not thought it worth while to tramp the Metropolis.

He was on his way then to see the dock-labourer, the one who had said that he was nothing but a village artist.

"If things get hopeless in your trade, come

to me," the man had told him. "I'll try to get you a job in the tobaccos."

He reached the dock-labourer's house, went up the rickety staircase, and knocked.

"Come in," said the rosy-cheeked little woman, "I s'pose it's George you want. He'll be back afore long. The baby didn't let him sleep till four, and then he overslept hisself. I s'pect he wouldn't get to the docks afore the men's took on."

"What's up with the kid *now?*" asked Jos.

"It's got the direa," explained the mother. "I'll 'ave to carry it to the 'ospital. The parish doctor says he can't do nothing for it. I've buried three children, and if this baby dies, I don't know whatever its father'll do, he's so took up with it."

The little woman began to cry, so Jos left the room in a hurry. He walked down Cambridge Street towards the Bethnal Green Museum, staring into windows as he went along, reading the last East End song, and looking at the latest East End advertisement. Presently he came to an eel-shop, where he watched eels being made into pies and soup. Almost unconsciously he fingered the Squirrel's sixpence, for he was famished. But he did not take the money out of his pocket. He walked on. At last he halted before a window, where an old woman, made of white plaster, advertised Pears' soap by washing a rebellious urchin with it. There his eyes fell on bottles, pots, and packets. He read, " This preparation forms a most nutritious food for infants, and is warranted to cure diarrhœa, as well as other infantine ailments."

Five minutes later he was back in the dock-labourer's room, holding out a yellow packet to the rosy-cheeked woman.

" There's some stuff for the kid," he said. " stuff what's good for its complaint."

" Kiss it," said the mother, " kiss it."

" Not if I knows it," said Jos. " Tell your husband I'll look in about six o'clock."

He went back to Cambridge Street, and straight on to the Bethnal Green Museum. There he turned through the garden gate, and stretched himself on a vacant seat. It would have been pleasant enough under the shade of the trees, if only he had not felt so hungry. The sky was blue, the flowers and grass made him think of the country. He filled his pipe with tobacco the deputy had given him the previous night, and took an old newspaper out of his pocket, one he had picked up in the street, but had not had time to read yet.

The first thing he saw was this :—

" On the 10th inst, John Datchett, Rector of Elmsworth, aged 56."

" So the rector's dead," he said. " If I'd posted that letter he'd never have got it."

He remembered the night on which he had been to say good-bye at the Rectory.

" I'm sorry you're going," the rector had told him.

Then the rector had pointed to a list of names in a frame, above the study fireplace, and had said, " There's just room there for me, Jos, sixteenth rector of this parish ! "

"So the rector's dead, " he repeated, as though he could scarcely believe it. " They said in the village his was a worse complaint than rheumatics."

He took the letter out of his pocket (the one to the clergyman of his parish which he had not posted), and as he tore it to bits there came over him a feeling of loneliness. He seemed to see his native place ; that quiet village, far away from a railway-station, full of primitive people. Somehow or other things had not gone well there lately. Labourers were out of work, farms were vacant, the shop was shut up, only one carpenter was wanted. Men had said that the land did not pay, and delegates had come about preaching strange doctrines. Certainly work was slack in the village ; that was why Jos had been forced to take his mother's savings out of the bank, and come to this great city.

" So the rector's dead," he said.

It was strange how that fact seemed to affect his spirits. He let his head fall on his chest, and in a half comatose state he thought of his mother in the churchyard, the only parent he had ever known, his one relation. He seemed to hear the church bells tolling for the rector, to see the ringers carrying the coffin on their shoulders through the village.

He was hungry. He had passed through the more active stages of that complaint, and now he had arrived at giddiness, emptiness, faintness.

How long he stayed in Bethnal Green garden it is impossible to say ; but when the sun was hottest he went to Victoria Park, and stretched himself on the grass.

There, then, he fell out of the ranks of the great army that goes marching on, heedless of stragglers, whose commander-in-chief is *laissez-faire*, upon whose banners "Grab who can," and "Let the devil take the hindermost," are written in large letters.

And the hounds, hunger and wretchedness, scenting him, led drink and crime to their prey; for drink and crime follow close on the steps of *laissez-faire's* army.

It was past six o'clock when he dragged himself up the dock-labourer's rickety staircase. No one seeing him would have recognised the smart young carpenter who, six months before, had arrived at Mrs. Elwin's house in tidy clothes, *with two boxes.* His dusty coat, his greasy hat, his dirty collar, and his old boots, made him look like a tramp.

He had reached that point of poverty at which it does not seem worth while to wash or to brush. His face was clean, and he had had his hair cut; but he had not shaved for nearly a week.

He had pawned everything the pawnbroker

would take, and although his razor was valueless,
he wanted the energy to shave himself.

" It's you, is it ? " he heard the dock-labourer
say, as he reached the landing.

"Come in, old chap. I'm downright grateful
to you for stopping that family music ! "

Jos went in. He sat down on a chair speechless.

"Whatever have you been doing with yourself ? " asked the dock-labourer ; "you look
famished."

But Jos did not hear him.

" Missus, run round the corner and fetch
some gin," said the dock-labourer. " He's
going off; he'll be clean gone in a minute."

When Jos came round again he found himself lying on the bed with his shirt open ; the
dock-labourer's wife was rubbing his feet, and
her husband was pouring gin down his throat.
Slowly he struggled back into consciousness ;
he drank some more gin, and new life seemed
to come into him.

"I guess I know what it is," he said, sitting
up, and staring at Mr. Chamberlain's orchid,
" I'm hungry."

" However did you get that direa mixture

then, if you hadn't no money?" asked the rosy-cheeked little woman.

Jos told her about the Squirrel's sixpence.

"Lor!" said the mother, turning away to look at the baby, "who'd have thought it!"

If Jos had wished to make friends of the mammon of unrighteousness, he could not have done better with that money. The mother could talk of nothing but the sleeping baby; and the father did not know how to express enough gratitude for the stuff which had (so he said) stopped the family music. They heaped Jos' plate with fried fish directly he was able to swallow anything, and made him drink still more of the gin that had brought new life into him.

"You meet me at Fenchurch Street station to-morrow," said the dock-labourer, "half-past six sharp. I think I can get you a job if you come along with me to-morrow morning."

Then he made Jos go out with him to have what he called "a bit of a spree." And they went through some back streets, across the Commercial Road, to a dancing-hall, a place not far from where the "Jolly Sailors" used to be, that favourite haunt of Jack Tars and foreigners.

They passed the bar, and went upstairs to a room where a number of girls and men were dancing. Two or three musicians sat at one end of the room, playing the latest East End galop on brass instruments, and on the sanded floor whirled girls and men, round and round, in and out, backwards and forwards, keeping time with the music.

"Does this young feller want a partner?" asked an old woman. Before Jos had time to answer a girl danced up to him. She took his face familiarly in her hands, and invited him to begin dancing.

Jos swore at her.

The dock-labourer laughed, and said, "We'll go downstairs if you don't care to dance."

Jos had been six months in London, but he had not entered a public-house before that night. As a boy he had been a teetotaler, to please his mother. It had never come into his head to break the pledge until he tasted that gin, that gin which had put new life into him. But, standing at the bar, among half-a-dozen friends of the dock-labourer, he tried another glass of spirits. Every one was anxious to treat him, for nowhere are men so generous as in a gin-palace; so he drank with this man and that. He experienced for the first time public-house hospitality, and listened to public-house gossip.

"Here's a queer customer coming in now," said the dock-labourer to Jos, as a pale-faced man, in shabby black, with a high hat, pushed through the swinging-doors, and came to the bar. "He get's his living making pictures; he's done one of the young lady here, behind the counter."

"The eyes is too small, and the waist's too big," exclaimed the barmaid, as the artist opened his portfolio, and exhibited a pen-and-ink sketch of her loveliness. "What do you say?" she asked turning to Jos, who as a new-comer had attracted her notice.

"I don't see no likeness," said Jos.

He went away to a table and lighted his pipe; certainly it was pleasanter to smoke there than in the doss-house. Every one was pleased to see him, and he had been alone so long that he enjoyed any welcome.

Presently the pale-faced man joined him, and said, "Maybe you've a sweetheart what you want painted!"

And Jos, the silent Jos, began to talk about Polly, to expatiate on the prettiness of his sweetheart. The gin he had been drinking helped him to see Polly in the little house they had so often talked about, it removed all difficulties, and showed him a time fast approaching, when he would have his tools safely out of the pawn shop, regular work, and good wages.

" I'd like to draw your sweetheart," said the artist; " from all you say, she must be a Wenus ! "

CHAPTER X.

WORK AT THE DOCKS.

HALF-PAST six o'clock the following morning found Jos at Fenchurch Street station. Half-past six is an unpleasant hour in that part of the city. The streets look greasy. There are not enough people about to enliven the houses. Shops have shutters up; untidy girls are scrubbing doorsteps; no one is there, except men on their way to work, old women going to market, and that scum of the populace who sleep in any hole they can, and live in any way they may; bleating sheep and lowing cattle are being driven along by butchers; yawning policemen are talking over a suicide here, a murder there; lean dogs are acting as scavengers; ragged children are seeking breakfast in dust heaps and gutters. The damp morning air is adding to the unpleasant smells in the atmosphere.

Little wonder that public-houses entice customers!

Before Jos reached Fenchurch Street station he had had "a glass of something to raise his spirits," for the dock-labourer had lent him a shilling, and the gin had done him so much good the previous evening, that he thought it wise to begin the day with the same remedy.

He found the train for Tidal Basin crowded with dock-labourers, all on their way to the Albert and Victoria Docks, where about one thousand men find employment.

It is reckoned that twenty thousand Londoners call themselves dock-labourers; of which number nearly the half is daily turned away to swell the number of the unemployed, to seek, by fair means or foul, a living.

Ten thousand! Just the number of that upper ten, about which people are so fond of talking!

A lowest ten, with wives and children!

"Tumble in," said Jos' friend to him. "Mates, here's a new chum, come to the docks to see if he can pick up a living!"

The carriage held about forty men, all untidy, unshaven, hungry people. A few had food tied up in pocket-handkerchiefs, one or two had bottles sticking out of their pockets. All had unbrushed hair, muddy boots, filthy hands, and dirty faces; some were sleeping, some were smoking, three or four were trying to laugh at the others.

"Wake up, Jim," said a young man, nudging an older companion. "You're always snoozing when you're not at work, old feller."

Jim raised his head, and gave a bovine glance at the person speaking to him. Then he let his body fall forward, and snoozed again.

"'Ave you 'eard what we unemployed's got to do Jubilee day?" continued the same young man, turning to the others.

"What then?"

"We've got to walk two and two down Cheapside afore the Queen; we've got to do penance in white sheets and candles; so I've read in the newspapers."

Then the men began to sing:—

"Starving on the Queen's highway."

The carriage was full of stale tobacco. All the windows were up. The men seemed to enjoy the stuffiness, to relish the smell and taste of it. But Jos, whose lungs still had some traces of country air in them, felt stifled. He sat upright, with his hands in his pockets, silent, looking steadily in front of him. His attitude towards the public was one of silence; he listened to conversation, but seldom said more than "yes" and "no." He could talk if he chose; in fact, he was sometimes surprised when he heard himself talking, for, like many uneducated men, he knew more than he was conscious of knowing; but he preferred to sit still and listen, to see and hear, and keep quiet.

At each station fresh passengers jumped in; and as they could not sit down, room was made for them in the centre of the carriage, against the windows, or on the knees of other men. It was "Ulloa, Tom!" and "Well, Bill!" at every platform, a desire to share tobacco, to show kindness, and receive favours. These men exist by the generosity of their fellows; and the only good thing that comes of being unemployed is " I help you, and you help me, because we've no place in society." This is the *one*, the *only* good thing among the legion of evils which are the outcome of enforced idleness. For loss

9

of self-respect, bitterness, the loosening of all social restraints, the lifting of that dam called Civilisation which keeps the passions of men from making beasts of them, are the results of telling a human being, "there is no work for you to do, you are not wanted."

At Tidal Basin all the men turned out of the train, and left the station. They went towards the docks, and some stopped at a public-house on the way, letting the others press on to the gates, where hundreds of men already stood waiting. Is any artist in need of a subject for his next Academy picture? If so, he had better visit the dock gates some early morning, and watch the men "taken on.'

By the gates of the Albert and Victoria Docks stand policemen, who keep order while the men pass into a covered pen, pass through to *beg* for that which Prince Bismarck (the wisest statesman in Europe) tells us they have a right to *demand*, to crave, as a favour, the boon of slaving all day, in order to carry home to wives and children a little money.

Through that pen went Jos, with his friend. Presently the labour-master came there. He held in his hand a note-book, also some etickets.

His face was a study for any artist. He spoke
to the men as only a labour-master is capable
of speaking, as only hungry, unemployed beings
are spoken to by their fellow-creatures. Yet
the men would have licked the dust off his
boots for a job; would have worshipped him
as a god if only he had said, "By doing me
homage you shall have work."

Thin dirty hands went up to this labour
Zeus, thin starved faces said, "O mighty one,
have mercy on us!"

Will no artist paint him? Has no artist
sympathy enough with suffering humanity to
visit the dock gates some early morning, and
afterwards show Christian England what it is
to be "'ungry"?

But why should any artist waste his time
there? The upper ten would only turn away
from the sorrows of that lowest ten if painted,
and say, "How vulgar! how disgusting!"

Jos was "taken on." He followed the dock-
labourer up a long stretch of ground, into some
large warehouses, where huge wooden casks
full of tobacco stood ready to be weighed
and tested. Enormous bales of tobacco were
piled one upon another, waiting for merchants.

Tobacco leaves littered the floor, and everywhere was a smell of tobacco. Through open doors he could see men tying leaves of it into bundles for samples, sorting good leaves from bad ones, testing and tasting it. And every man he met was chewing tobacco.

He was told to help move some bales, and the dock-labourer gave him a lesson in lifting and carrying, which he found difficult to put into practice. He was not accustomed to hard, manual labour, and he was clumsy at it. But the men helped him. When he was told to lend a hand weighing hogsheads, to tilt them into the scales, and knock their rings off and on, they let him drive in the iron bar for testing. His friend went out tallying; but the other dock-labourers were just as willing to show him everything, and thanks to them he did not get "blown up" by the overseer, or reported as a "duffer" to the labour-master.

It was the same work all day long, lifting, carrying, weighing, testing, sampling, and chewing tobacco. Hour followed hour, with nothing to break the monotony, except half an hour off for lunch, when the men had a dip in the river, smoked, and ate anything they had to eat.

It *did* seem a shame to waste all that tobacco ! Spoilt bales were burnt, sweepings were taken to the furnace, the men were not allowed to carry a bit away, although not a few men were very hungry.

At last the day's work was done, and the men trooped out of the gates with a few shillings in their pockets. Some went straight to the station, but many, and among these Jos, stopped at the public-house, where they found others who had not been "taken on," who had been hanging about the gates all day, hoping that the contractors would call on more hands.

"I'm going on tramp to-morrow," said a strong-looking fellow. "My missus is ill, and maybe if I clear off, she'll get summat from the parish. P'raps, mates, you'll oblige me with a few coppers. I'll do the same by you when I've got the money."

He walked from man to man, holding out a ragged cap. Jos dropped a penny into it. As the money clinked against other coins, Jos thought of a story he had heard in his native village, a sort of myth, handed on from father to son, and only half believed in by any one. It was said that a tramp had once been found dead in the woods there, and that the doctor's verdict had been " death from starvation."

"What's it like on tramp?" he asked the owner of the ragged cap, who was tying up the pennies in the corner of his pocket-handkerchief.

" Like ? Well, mate, you sleep in a ditch, and there's nothing to pay for it ; you get a job if you can ; if not, you snare a rabbit or steal a chicken. Children run away if they see you coming, and women treat you as if you was old Nick. Often you're had up afore a magistrate, and you come off worst when a parson's on the bench. But you pick up something harvesting, and it's best to go if your missus is dying—least-ways, I can't stay by and do nothing."

"Come along," said a man to Jos ; "we'll be late for the train if you aren't quick."

It was a noisy company that went back from Tidal Basin that evening, a very different one from that which had come down in the early morning. Men sang, shouted, laughed, quarrelled for seats, and used bad language. Jos fell asleep, and did not wake up until he reached Fenchurch Street station. Then he rubbed his eyes, and for the first time realised his surroundings. He was a dock-labourer.

He looked like his mates, and they looked like him. As he left the carriage, with Jim and Bill rollicking beside him, he saw people turn away ; he felt that he had dropped to a lower level of things than he had been in before, that there is a great difference between a carpenter in good work and a dock-labourer. He pulled his hat over his eyes, as though he did not wish to be recognised. Outside the station he wished the others good-bye, and went away by himself towards the common lodging-house.

So this was what he had come to !

Well, he could not help it. It was not his fault. Yesterday he was a beggar, ill, penniless, friendless. To-day he had, at any rate, a few shillings in his pocket, and the men, though rough, had been good to him.

Was it his fault ?

After all, he had had *some* luck, for he had been "taken on," while numbers of other men had been obliged to hang about all day, doing nothing.

He caught sight of himself in a shop window, and turned away. His coat had a tear across the back, he had on no collar, only a bit of old flannel shirt tied round his neck. His boots were full of grit, which made his feet bleed. He could see blood oozing through the holes in his boots on to the pavement.

Well, he would just turn in somewhere, and have a glass of something before he went back to the doss-house. Three pennyworth of gin would cost less than supper, and be better for him. There was a small public-house close by ; he would have a drop there, then go straight to bed, for his bones ached, and he was so stiff that he could scarcely lift his hand up. He found it hard to drag one foot after the other. At the door of the public-house crouched two old women, like sphinxes. Wrinkles were cut deep in their tough yellow skin, thin locks of grey hair fell over their red inflamed eyelids. Their bony hands clasped their tattered petticoats. They looked on the ground heedless of passers-by, except when a man or woman dropped them a halfpenny. There they sit day and night, those sphinxes. And there they will stay until *Laissez-faire* and his army lose the day, until his banners are seized by the enemy.

Jos went in.

Half-a-dozen girls and men were there drinking ; pewter pots passed from hand to hand. Obscene jokes were followed by sensual laughter. The company was noisy, and the publican encouraged it to become noisier.

Jos had his glass of spirits. And then, growing reckless, he clinked the shillings in his pocket. He stood this man and that woman a drink. He leant his arms on the bar, and listened while the girls and men he had treated sang " For he's a jolly good feller."

At last he left the place, and went towards the common lodging-house.

" Shall I take you home ? " he heard a voice asking.

" Why ? What ? " he said. " Who is it ? "

" The folks is all laughing at you," said the Squirrel. " You can't walk straight. What have you been about ? "

" Work at the docks."

" Yes," said the Squirrel, looking wisely at him. " Come home, Jos."

PART II.

◆

CHAPTER XI.

THE CLASS-LEADER COMES TO TEA.

"WELL, Polly," said Mrs. Elwin, a few weeks after the Jubilee gathering, "considering William Ford's kind enough to show us the Mint, I think you *might* put on your best bonnet."

Polly went silently upstairs, and did as her mother suggested. Afterwards she followed Mrs. Elwin, who was clad in her Sunday garments, out of the home, through the streets to the Mint.

"I'm all of a fluster," whispered her mother, as they passed the sentinels, and reached a gate guarded by two policemen. "To think William Ford goes in and out here every day where they make so much money!"

" It's a beautiful place," said Polly, looking
at the smooth green grass, the pond with water-
lilies on the surface, and the tall houses. " It's
like a palace."

Mrs. Elwin settled the shawl on her shoulders,
shook out her purple silk dress, and inquired of
a policeman,—

" What's the way in, sir ? "

" Have you an order ? "

" Yes."

" Through that door, then," he said, replac-
ing the order in its envelope, and pointing to
the entrance. " A party's just gone there. If
you're quick, you'll be in time to join it."

" I wish William Ford was here," Mrs. Elwin
told her daughter, while she walked up the
broad path, trailing her silk gown, and fidgetting
with the pin attached to the portrait of the late
lamented Mr. Elwin ; " my heart's beating like
anything."

" He said we'd be sure to see him somewhere about," said Polly, " though he couldn't
leave his work to join us. Come along,
mother."

So they went through the entrance into a
room full of heraldic signs, adorned with

numismatic mysteries, where they signed their names in a book. Then they followed the guide and some Americans, who were "doing" the Mint together with the Tower of London, and a few other places of interest.

There was a good deal to be seen just then, for gold was being made into those half-sovereigns which bore such a convenient resemblance to gilded sixpences. First of all they were taken into a room, where bars of gold were being coined, and stamped by machinery. Here the Americans brought out their Bædekers, and made remarks to the guide in nasal accents. One calculated he would like to know how much metal was there altogether. Another guessed the answers he received were not quite what he wanted, and was sure that the Mint could not be "done" without more information.

Then the guide showed them some five-pound pieces, which were being made to celebrate the Jubilee, coins on which Her Most Gracious Majesty is represented with a sort of night-cap at the back of her head, a design that has no precedent in heraldry, however much nineteenth century taste may admire it.

" I guess she looks queer," said an American, taking a five-pound piece gingerly between his fingers, and handing it to Mrs. Elwin.

" How's she done ? " whispered Polly to her mother.

" Done ! " exclaimed Mrs. Elwin, shocked by such an impious desire for information. " She's god-like, Polly. How *can* you ask such a question ? "

The words were scarcely out of her mouth when William Ford joined them. The white cotton clothes he had on made him look so different from the man Polly was accustomed to see in chapel and at class meetings, that she scarcely recognised him. She did not recover from her astonishment until she heard her mother say,—

" Oh, Mr. Ford, who'd have thought the world held such a lot of money ! "

The philosophy of clothes remains yet to be written. Carlyle has only laid down the first principles of it, given a few hints to that member of the other sex who will one day write a whole system of clothes philosophy, a work that will rival in length and suggestiveness the productions of Monsieur Comte himself, and meet with the same world-wide recognition as his philosophy.

There is a favourite East End song, beginning :—

> "Captain Cuff! Captain Cuff!
> You may know him by his collar,
> Though he's not worth half-a-dollar!"

If such a man may be known by a bit of starched linen round his neck, another may be much more successfully diagnosed by a cotton coat. Polly saw before her eyes a young man who had been disguised by his Methodist garments, who in his cotton clothes, surrounded by bars of gold and glittering half sovereigns, was not at all bad-looking.

The guide walked on with the Americans, leaving William Ford to explain the machinery to Mrs. Elwin and her daughter. This he did, in imposing sentences. Mrs. Elwin enjoyed his explanations much as the old lady enjoyed that beautiful word Mesopotamia in her clergyman's sermon, not knowing how easy it is to talk about things, and how difficult it is to understand them. She was aware that he received over a hundred a year in the Mint, that he had been there as a boy, and might stay there, if he liked, until he approached senility. And she could not help thinking,— indeed she felt convinced,—that Providence had placed him in such an enviable position because he was a godly young Methodist. She ignored the fact (perhaps she was not aware of it) that such places often pass from father to son, that the Treasury appoints men to them for other reasons than godliness. As she followed William Ford past bars of gold, and watched half sovereigns gliding through his fingers, she thanked God that England held such godly young men as the class-leader, apparently quite unconscious that she was worshipping the golden calf instead of Jesus of Nazareth!

Polly listened to all the leader had to say with downcast eyes and blushes. And when she heard her mother's request, "Do come to tea this evening," she seconded the invitation by a modest glance, that sent the blood coursing up into the young man's high forehead.

On the way home the mother and daughter did not talk much. For weeks they had had an open secret. They had, in fact, become aware that Polly could, if she liked, marry her class-leader. He had been several times

lately to Mrs. Elwin's house, and it needed no
Jew now to see that he was "sweet upon
Polly." He said nothing about himself, but
his sighs and looks were quite sufficient.
Sometimes, in class, he asked after Jos.
Oftener still he spoke against the Church, and
extolled Methodists. He was such a very
godly young man, that it never entered Polly's
head to suspect his line of conduct was not
quite honest. Of course he was bound to
put her spiritual welfare before her temporal
happiness, to point out that, poor, or rich,
a churchman was not a fit husband for a
Wesleyan-Methodist.

This he did to Polly in class. When Mrs.
Elwin was present he said nothing at all about
Jos, and Polly (who was a little afraid of her
mother) was silent about her legitimate, and
her illegitimate, lover.

The little sitting-room looked clean and fresh
when the godly young man arrived in it. It
had lately been papered and varnished. White
curtains were in the windows. Coloured paper
adorned the fireplace. Mrs. Elwin had brought
out her best china teacups, also a bottle of rum
that Uncle Cohen had given her as a Christmas

present. (Mrs. Elwin did not really enjoy her tea unless it had rum in it.)

Mary Anne carried a kettle there from the kitchen, and went away quite unconscious that a drama was being played before her eyes, one quite as interesting as any that she read about in dog-eared novelettes. If a lord or lady had come to tea, Mary Anne would have seen in each aristocratic action, in every aristocratic glance, enough romance to suffice for the whole aristocracy. People without titles she thought commonplace, unless they belonged to that wonderful order of beings who hover betwixt earth and heaven, namely, actors and actresses, who are capable of changing from kings to dukes, from queens to duchesses, according to their good pleasure, who wear such lovely dresses, and speak such beautiful language. Polly's lovers were no more to Mary Anne than the butcher's boy; only possible husbands, who would introduce their wives into unromantic homes, in which there would be "a deal of work to do" for them and their children. Besides, Mary Anne was quite unconscious of the fact that the class-leader might be looked upon as a rival of Polly's legitimate lover, one who in a story book would shoot Jos, or be shot by the young carpenter. Had she not witnessed love-scenes in the parlour between Polly and Jos, which scarcely rivalled in interest those she herself played with the butcher's boy? As to that ugly young man William Ford, why should not he come there to tea, just as the Jew Cohen came to dinner "of a Sunday"?

Mrs. Elwin was very silent all teatime; she let Polly and the class-leader monopolise the whole conversation. But she watched the young man's face, and while watching she made up her mind about something,—something that took away her appetite, and led her to tilt the bottle of rum into her tea-cup, when she saw that William Ford's eyes were fixed on the pretty Methodist.

After tea, directly Mary Anne had cleared away the tea things, and Polly had gone upstairs to her work, Mrs. Elwin folded her hands on her lap, and cleared her throat.

" I'm sure, Mr. Ford," she said, in a voice slightly agitated, " I've much to thank you for. It's sad when a girl's left with but one parent, and that a lone woman like myself. After

the late-lamented Mr. Elwin died, leaving me
with Polly in a house like this, I often asked
myself whatever would become of us. I've
strange folks here at times as lodgers. I've
had so many Jews here at once, that one of
my rooms has been made into a synagogue
without my knowing it. I've had six Moham-
medans standing their feet in tubs of water at
the back, because they couldn't say their
prayers till they'd done their heathen habits.
I've had black men, what have run up and
downstairs in nothing but their night shirts.
I've civilised many of em. I don't mean to say
as I've made 'em into Methodists, God alone
could do that ; but I *do* mean to say as I've
done my duty here as a landlady."

The leader twisted a hair of his moustache
between his finger and thumb without speaking.

" I'm sure," continued Mrs. Elwin, " I've to
thank you for the trouble you've taken with
Polly in class. I always says to her, ' You
ought to thank God, Polly, becos He's given
you, what haven't a father, a godly class-
leader.' Though I say it, as oughtn't, seeing
she's my own daughter, she's as good and

modest a girl as ever set foot anywhere, let alone in a house like this, full of heathen and heretics."

The mother paused, overcome by her feelings. " I'm sure," she went on to say presently, " I'm sure you'll understand how it goes against me to see that young man Joseph Coney, what hasn't a penny he can lay his hands on, coming here after Polly. Never tell me young men can't get work if they ain't lazy. I'm sure he did something bad down in the place where he comes from, and he's been doing bad things since he came to London."

The leader let his eyes fall on the carpet, and said slowly, " He's church. I don't think she's a right to marry a man who isn't a Methodist."

Mrs. Elwin gave a start. The colour came into her comely cheeks, and her blue eyes glistened. She drew in her breath for half a minute.

"That's just it!" she exclaimed; "that's just it! When I think of Polly marrying a man what isn't a Methodist I go all of a creep; and I'm sure it would make the late-lamented

Mr. Elwin turn in his coffin if he knowed of it."

The leader rose up slowly.

"Pray for the light of God on it, Mrs. Elwin," he said, in a solemn voice. "Pray for the light of God on it."

Directly the door had closed upon the godly youth Mrs. Elwin nodded her head in a satisfied way, and went to find Polly. "Polly," she said, seating herself on the bed in the little room upstairs, where her daughter was busy with needlework, "I've been talking with William Ford about something I've had on my mind, something what's been a sore trouble to me this long while. Polly, did you never think how wrong it would be to marry a man what isn't a Methodist?"

The girl turned to look at her mother. She had listened to other arguments. She had heard, "If you marry a man what hasn't a penny to bless himself with, you'll come to selling lemon-kali in the streets, and live in a block where folks has only one washhouse." And, "I don't say as you should keep your servant, but I *do* say as it's flying in the face of Providence to marry a man like Joseph

Coney." She had never heard *this* argument from her mother before, only from her class-leader.

" All I can say is, if you do it, you'll break my heart, Polly," her mother continued. " Remember, you've only got *one* parent."

" I can't give Jos up," the girl said at last. " I knew he was church when he asked me to marry him. I knew he wasn't a Methodist."

" Ah! well," said her mother, in a reproachful voice, " you'll be sorry when you've *two* dead parents."

Mrs. Elwin went downstairs to the kitchen, and there she gave vent to her feelings in scolding her maidservant. The laziness of domestics was one of her favourite topics. Mary Anne worked from five in the morning until late at night; but in a house full of heathen many things gave food for grumbling. Mrs. Elwin's tongue was a scourge in the kitchen ; and that evening it lashed so hard, that the butcher's boy, who found Mary Anne crying after the operation, begged the girl to give notice there and then, and come to live with him.

" 'Tain't the likes of you I'm going to live with!" said Mary Anne, tossing her head.

The poor lad left the house disconcerted.

Meanwhile Polly continued her sewing. She pricked her fingers ; red spots marked the white stuff on her knee. She looked at the spots, and said,

" I wish Jos would go away ; I wish he'd go back to the country." Poor Polly !

Natures like hers are incapable of deep feeling; they always love their fellow-creatures in a qualified manner. They vacillate from pillar to post ; and stay longest at the point where they discover their own interest. " I wish Jos would go away," sighed the poor little Methodist ; " I wish he'd go back to the country."

CHAPTER XII.

THE Jubilee was over and done with. Strange to say, no one was very sorry; even Her Most Gracious Majesty was completely exhausted, overwhelmed with fêtes and presents. It had failed to bring work into the country; for the little spurt given by it to employment had vanished like a pebble thrown into the sea, had died away in the ocean of unemployed misery.

Every morning Jos went to the tobaccos, and brought back with him a few shillings. He began rather to like the doss-house. Instead of stealing away to the door, as he had done that first evening, he now smoked with the other men; he learnt the art of gambling; the deputy showed him how to begin, and the deputy's wife stood him a drink when he needed encouragement. She seemed to "fancy" the young carpenter, and allowed him to keep the "slip" at the top of the house, instead of "turning in" with the other lodgers. Sometimes she gave him a cup of coffee before he started for the docks, when she came downstairs at six o'clock, to take the place of her husband, who then went to bed, leaving her in charge of the doss-house. She was a woman with a strong arm and a brazen countenance. She had had a baby once, and she had sold it for eighteenpence.

No one could starve in the doss-house, although all were very far below "the line of poverty," and most had touched "the line of starvation." They shared scraps and lent halfpence. Jos let the Squirrel cater for him. She waited for him every night at the entrance of the doss-house; and directly he turned the corner of the street she darted back into the kitchen. Five minutes later he had his supper; then he either fell asleep, or found his way into a public-house. The Squirrel watched him. If he slept, she went to bed; if he left the doss-house, she sometimes followed him down the street, and waited outside a public-house until midnight.

He soon became acquainted with his fellow-lodgers, men and women who came there again and again, just as vagrants frequent casual wards, and habitual drunkards pass their Sundays at Bow Street.   Sometimes a stranger appeared amongst them, as Jos had done, sent by a policeman.   The stranger either went away next day, or settled in there to play " Man and Homan."

One morning Jos overslept himself. A heavy fog made the slip dark ; he could not believe it was morning when he woke up ; his head ached. Something unpleasant had, he knew, taken place the previous day; he did not remember what it was exactly, but he thought that a policeman had threatened to run him in, that he had had a fall somewhere.   Stains of blood were on the dirty sheets, and round his knee was a dirty, blood-stained pocket-handkerchief.

He stood up, dressed himself, and stumbled downstairs.   There he found the deputy's wife scrubbing the kitchen. It was eight o'clock ; the men had been taken on at the docks half an hour before.   He had no chance in the tobaccos, but he might get a job on some ship perhaps ; so he went to Fenchurch Street, and took the train to Tidal Basin. He was alone in the railway carriage; and sitting there he wondered what had happened the night before, where he had been, and who had been with him.

As he left the station, and went down the wooden steps, he met Robinson, a man who called himself an anarchist.

Robinson held in his hand *The Britain*, and his face glowed with young authorship. He seized Jos by the arm, and pointed to some verses on the last sheet. Then he waved *The Britain* above his head, and rushed forward to show the porters his success. He already saw himself an acknowledged poet! Not the Poet Laureate, he thought nothing of people like that; not even William Morris, who is only a Socialist; but the poet of the people, a Sims imbued with Anarchist principles. Robinson wore a fur cap and a short blue jacket. He earned his living at the docks, and sometimes played an harmonium in the streets, to which he sang songs of liberty and justice. He belonged to a small Anarchist Club, and had once shaken hands with Krapotkin. Socialism was, he said, milk-and-water stuff; Anarchism alone could bring deliverance.

Jos looked after him for a minute, vaguely wondering why he was so excited, then passed on to the dock gates. No one was there, so he went to the public-house. Some men were playing pitch-and-toss outside it, whiling away the time by winning halfpence, and giving them back again. Jos turned into the bar, and ordered some gin-and-water.

He stood there staring at the coloured glasses, thinking his knee was stiff, wondering how he had cut it. Presently a man joined him.

" This dock's the beastliest place I've ever come to," said the new-comer to Jos. " I've been all over the world, and I've never seen anything to equal it. Now I'm sacked because I'm slow at tilting them d— hogsheads. As to the men, they've got the knack, but they take care not to show it."

" Did you come here with a character ? " inquired Jos.

" Yes, from the colonel of my regiment."

" Oh, then you'll never get on. The men here won't put up with characters. They're always shy of a man what's recommended, and show him nothing."

" Why's that ? "

" They're jealous. The labour-master puts men what's recommended into the best places, so the others make it difficult for 'em to get on ; they show 'em nothing."

The new-comer gave a groan, and sank down on a seat by the bar. He was a tall wellbuilt man, very strong, with twenty years of work still in him.

" I've served my Queen and my country for fifteen years," he said, "and this is what I've come to. I've had bullets whizzing round my head, I've had fevers, I've nearly died of thirst in Egypt, and now I can't get a job anywhere, not even as a dock-labourer. Here goes my character."

He took the colonel's letter out of his pocket, tore it into bits, put it in his mouth, chewed it, spat it on the ground, and stamped on it.

" Have a glass ? " Jos suggested.

The man shook his head. He looked at Jos for a minute, and said as if to himself, " The poor devil's killing himself with spirits." Then he left the place, and the doors swung to after him.

Jos stayed in the public-house all day, drinking and smoking. Once or twice he went to the dock gates, but no contractor came down to call on more men ; he was not wanted. He sat at the bar, on a narrow wooden seat, saturating his body, and deadening his intelligence with spirits.

At last the dock-labourers trooped out from their work, and the place was filled with thirsty men. Among them was the man whose acquaintance Jos had made on Mile End Waste the day that the Queen had gone down there to open the People's Palace.

"Hulloa!" he said, seeing Jos. "Why weren't you here this morning ? "

" I overslept myself."

The man looked at him, then came to the wooden seat and sat down. " Did your father drink ? " he asked slowly.

"What's that to you ? " inquired Jos.

" If he didn't your mother did," the man said with emphasis. " I've never seen a feller fall to drink as you've done, unless it had come down from father to son, and was in the constitootion. Drink seems just to soak into you."

" Mind your own business," said Jos, sullenly.

" Come along of me," the man said, getting

up. "My missus is always asking after you. Come along of me, old chap. Don't be foolish."

But Jos took no notice. He stuck to the bar like a limpet. As the dock-labourer said— drink seemed to soak into him. By the time he left the public-house his pockets were empty, but for a return ticket. And he would have sold that had any one wanted it ; although, if he had done so, his bed must have been a ditch, somewhere between Tidal Basin and Fenchurch Street station.

It was late when he reached the doss-house. Most of the lodgers had gone to bed, and the deputy was fast asleep by the fireplace. But the Squirrel was there, watching his supper. He came shivering to the fire, and leant his arm against the wall. He looked at the flames blazing up the chimney, and at the tin pot into which the Squirrel was putting scraps of bread and potatoes.

The strong lights and shadows fell on the little sharp face of the deputy, who lay back in his chair, with his hands clasped, and his legs stretched out. They showed the " 'ungry " man in the corner on a heap of rags, a bed he

received gratis; they lighted up the great
dark eyes of the Squirrel. She would not be a
child much longer; and in those eyes were
depths of passion that might one day lead her
into trouble. Passion was latent in them at
present; but tender motherly love, such as a
child lavishes on its favourite doll or on a pet
animal, gave them pathos. She turned to look
at Jos; and as she looked her face became full
of solicitude. It was easy to see that he had
been drinking, and the Squirrel felt sorry for
him. She pushed back the short thick hair
that fell over her face, and carried the tin of
soup to a table.

Jos followed her.

While he ate his supper she stood by his
side in silence. Her dress scarcely reached
below the knee. A dirty pinafore and a small
triangular shawl completed her toilette. There
was something foreign about her appearance.
She looked Italian, not English. At last she
said, " How's your knee, Jos ? "

" Stiffish."

" Let me see." She knelt down on the
floor, and carefully turned the trouser up above
the knee. The pocket-handkerchief had stuck

to the flesh. She could not loosen it. She jumped up, and left the kitchen. When she came back he had finished his supper, and lay with his head on the table. She knelt down again, and placed a basin full of hot water beside him.

Softly, with wonderful patience, she bathed the knee. Jos let his hand fall on her head. Her face flushed scarlet. For one second she fixed her great dark eyes on him. Then she gently moved his hand away, and went on with her work.

" I'll help you to bed," she said, after his knee was bound up again with a bit of linen.

Leaning heavily on her shoulder he went up the staircase. He wished her good-night when he reached the slip. He threw himself upon the bed, too tired to undress, too stupefied by drink to think if he was inside or outside the blankets. He could not go to the tobaccos the following day, for he had no money. He thought a job at St. Kit's or the London Docks would be better than a long walk to Tidal Basin ; besides, he did not care for the men at the Victoria Docks to know that he was penniless, he thought that he would begin again

among strangers.   So he went to the gates of
the London Docks, and when the bell began to
ring he was lifted almost off his feet by thousands of hungry applicants for work.   The tide
of men carried him into a broad yard, where
contractors take on hands, and a labour-master
watches over the company's interests.

Years hence, when children read in lesson-
books about the Age of Competition, the docks
will be given as an illustration of the competitive system after it reached a climax.   Boys
and girls will read that thousands of Englishmen fought daily at the dock gates for tickets ;
that starving men behind pressed so hard on
starving men in front, that the latter were nearly
cut in two by the iron railings which kept them
from work ; that contractors were mauled by
hungry men ; that brick-bats and stones were
hurled at labour-masters by men whose families
were starving.

"And all that time," the children will say,
"England pretended to worship the Son of a
carpenter, to follow One, Who, if He had lived
in the nineteenth century, would certainly have
been found beside the dock gates instead of at
drawing-room meetings, and in churches!"

Jos had no chance there that morning. An east wind was blowing up the river, and the ships in the harbour were few. He might get a job another day; even that was not likely. For he stood alone among a crowd of loafers, corner-men, and thieves; he had no friend to help him. Besides, his face had that look of soddenness which means intemperance, and his clothes hung loosely on his limp arms and legs. He did not seem worth hiring, and the contractors passed him by without a ticket. The bell stopped ringing, and the men trooped off to the other places where hands are taken on during the day. Jos went to the fifth gate. He stood about there all the morning, watching the men climb up the wooden palings when a contractor came along, seeing tickets put through the gate and grabbed at. He began to realise that a job could only be obtained by physical strength, that he had no chance until his leg was well again. His pockets were empty; so he went back to the doss-house. He passed the rest of the day playing "man and homan" with two or three gamblers who lent him some halfpence.

CHAPTER XIII.

TRAFALGAR SQUARE.

WEEKS and months passed by.

He got a job sometimes at the London Docks, or at St. Kit's, but the shillings he earned were very casual, and, like all insecure things, they had a demoralising influence. Once he took his clothes out of pawn, and made up his mind to visit the pretty Methodist. But he turned back before he reached her home. He was afraid to face Mrs. Elwin, afraid that Polly would ask,—

"Jos, have you got any work yet?"

He had not forgotten his sweetheart; but he kept his thoughts away from her memory as a painful thing, although her memory just prevented him from sinking.

"You've not 'ad 'em out long, Mister," the old woman said, when he took the clothes back next day to the pawn-shop.

He seemed suddenly to know that he would

never need the clothes again ; and seizing them
from the woman he went to Houndsditch, where
he sold them in the Old Clothes Market. The
money he received for them burnt in his pocket.
He longed to get rid of it. So he treated the
Squirrel that night to a music-hall entertain-
ment.

They had seats in the pit ; and the Squirrel
became so excited that she worked her way up
to the footlights. She leant her arms on the
low stage, and seemed to drink in the music.
Her great eager eyes followed the movements
of the dancers ; and she sang every chorus,
beating time to it with her fists and feet.

The songs were chiefly political. " England
for the English, and Heaven for us All," was
encored over and over again. The chorus
expressed a fervent wish to "chuck" the
foreigner back to " his own dear native land,"
and the galleries stood up to wave their hand-
kerchiefs as the singer retired from the platform. " The Prince and the Actress " was a
failure, for the reciter dried up in the most
pathetic part. And " There's One more River,
there's One more River to pass," did not attract
much notice.

The Squirrel quivered with excitement during the whole performance. Jos drank beer, and watched her.

They had drifted into the strangest relationship. Seeing them together one would have fancied that they were brother and sister; although she had foreign features, and eyes in which were left some faint traces of a sunny climate, while he was a commonplace young Englishman. As she trotted along beside him on their way home that night he took little notice of her. (He was thinking of the pretty Methodist.) He looked on her as a kind little thing, better than nothing. Sometimes he gave her a caress, much as a man lets his hand fall on the head of a spaniel. From this she always shrank away. Then she came back again, with a motherly look on her face, which was almost ridiculous.

It is impossible to say in what way she regarded Jos. But from the time he set foot in the doss-house she ministered unceasingly to his comforts. She worked for him day and night, she followed him about, she spoke to him in a motherly way that was quite funny.

The work he had to do at the London
Docks and St. Kit's was much the same as
in the tobaccos. Lifting, weighing, testing,
and tallying went on there all day with cease-
less monotony. Once or twice he was put on
night-work, then he received an extra penny
per hour ; and from eight in the evening till
eight in the morning he carried bales of wool
up to the top of huge warehouses for a north
light, and carried them back again to be for-
warded to merchants. He did not get much
night-work, for the preference-men would work
twenty-four and thirty-six hours at a stretch
rather than forfeit it. But once or twice while
the wool sales were on he got a job, and then
he went up and downstairs all night with a
truck.

When it was time for breakfast, he sometimes walked to the end of the harbour before
he turned into the doss-house. He liked to
see the sun rising, it reminded him of things
down in his native village ; to watch the foreign
sailors, and hear their strange gibberish ; to
look at the big ships, the steamers "from
foreign parts," and the barges full of things
that the nation wanted. The warehouses

afforded him endless amusement. Floors covered with ivory, rooms filled with mammoth teeth, shelves holding mother-of-pearl,— all these excited his interest. Everything that people could want to eat, everything that people could care to drink, stood in those warehouses. And among all this wealth worked the hungriest set of men in England, while sleek merchants, who came to make bargains, were furnished with refreshments. It seemed to him a horrible injustice that men should see all these things, and move them about, while suffering from empty stomachs. He could not say *why* it was wrong exactly ; and he kept his thoughts to himself, for he was a very silent man, very much afraid of being laughed at.

The only person who could have thrown any light on the subject was his friend the dock-labourer, who preached on Mile End Waste, and talked like a book. But he did not go to see this man, for at that time he was not drinking.

Work got slack.

It was just then that the Squirrel said,—

" Why spend fourpence a night in the doss-house ? "

She had been selling fusees near Trafalgar Square, and had seen a number of vagrants camping out there at night, making beds of rags on the stone steps, and tents under the noses of policemen.

"Hundred of folks were there last night," she told Jos. "I heard a bobby say so. Let's sleep there, 'stead of in the doss-house."

"They'll run us in," said Jos.

"No they won't."

"It's a long way from there to the docks.'

"Yes, but we'll 'ave breakfast."

He was only half persuaded, but he joined her that night at Charing Cross. In the square he found an old acquaintance. This was Reeson, the carpenter, on his way to the workhouse.

Reeson was walking up and down with his hands in his pockets. His thin lips were close together; his square jaw showed the bones near the skin, bones on which was little flesh; his face looked bloodless; his grey hair stood out in stiff, short bristles, as a man's hair does when he is under the influence of some strong emotion. Sometimes he stopped to look at his wife, who sat on the stone ledge beneath one of the parapets.

Her hands were clasped about her knees, and she looked as if she would never cry again, not even at a pauper's funeral. By her side was a bundle, containing all the worldly goods she had left, a few old rags, two cards,—the Ancient Order of Druids, and the Supreme Order of Buffaloes,—and her dead children's photographs.

"You here?" said Reeson, when he saw Jos.

Then the two men began to tramp up and down the square in strange, silent fashion slowly, looking steadily into the distance.

Night came on.

Reeson stretched himself on the stone ledge beside his wife, and laid his head on the bundle that contained the photographs. Close by them was the Squirrel, curled up in a ball, with her big eyes fixed on Jos. Carriages and cabs rolled past, carrying people home from theatres and concerts.

Big Ben struck twelve.

Then the square began to fill rapidly with people. Tall policemen took up their station in it as sentinels. The law had said, "It is time to close public-houses;" and men and women, who had no other homes than gin-palaces, came to lie there on the wooden seats, the stone steps, and the ledges beneath the parapets. Some brought old bits of sacking and old blankets. Many spread out old newspapers, and wrapt themselves round with old sheets of advertisements. A few crept under tarpaulin tents, in which they had stowed away their children, with all the worldly goods of the family. Six hundred outcasts at length lay there quiet ; and as Jos walked up and down he heard sounds of heavy breathing, nothing else, unless some poor consumptive wretch commenced to cough, and spit blood on the pavement, or a child began to cry, thinking that its mother had left it alone in a strange country.

He went to the water, in which he could see the stars reflected. They danced up and down in mocking fashion, as though the universe had nothing to do with the earth, but to laugh at its littleness. He looked up at them. They were far off, and pitiless.

Then *he* laughed ; a bitter laugh that echoed round Nelson's monument, and died away among the pillars of the National Gallery. The noise attracted a policeman, who came up, and said a few warning words about vagrants.

He turned away, and walked towards the Squirrel. A great thirst was on him, a thirst that all the waters in the square would not quench, for spirits. He had eaten nothing the whole day. He was not hungry; but he felt that he *must* have some gin. He knew how the stuff would soak into his flesh, how it would deaden his consciousness.

The Squirrel had twopence.

He went to the place where she was curled up. Her eyes were shut; her little pale face had a smile on it. She was leaning against the stone wall, and smiling in her sleep over some dream of happiness.

He walked away slowly. As the clock struck one, he said,—

"Money's no use. They've shut the gin-shops."

He lay down on a bench, and turning his eyes on the ground, so that he could not see the stars that so mocked his distress, and laughed at his loneliness, he fell asleep. When he awoke his head felt hot, and his hands were feverish. He, too, had been dreaming. He had seen the old clergyman, John Datchett, standing by an open grave, reading out of a

book. Some one had said, "It's right to look
in on the coffin," and looking into that yawning
pit that held his mother, his one relation, he
had seen——

Then he woke up, shuddering.

Big Ben struck five, and grey dawn slowly
took the place of grim darkness. The buildings came out in distinct angles and squares,
the pillars showed lines and curves. Morning
crept out of night, and Big Ben marked its
growth by ticking births and deaths in seconds
and minutes.

At last the Squirrel came to the place where
he lay, and said,—

"It's time for breakfast."

His limbs were so stiff that he found it
almost impossible to stand upright. The damp
had settled in his joints, for hunger had weak-
ened him, and gin had made his sinews limp.
He followed the Squirrel with difficulty, and
warmed himself by a charcoal fire, while she
ordered two cups of coffee, and two slices of
bread-and-butter.

A small crowd had gathered in front of the
tent under which an old man was serving penny
breakfasts. Men who had been working since

two o'clock for the parish, labourers, flower-girls, and a decayed gentleman, stood there eating bread-and-butter, drinking weak tea or coffee.

"Take one cup, and you'll come again. Good tea and coffee. Best quality," the old man had put up on his tent; and his donkey rubbed its head against tender-hearted people, asking for crusts in return for bringing them breakfasts. When the decayed gentleman had finished he raised his hat to the flower-girls, and wished the old man "Good-morning." His coat was threadbare and greasy, his high collar had not seen soap-and-water for weeks; but he bowed with all the grace of *la haute noblesse*, just to show that he could bear poverty with a dignified presence. The flower-girls laughed at him. If he had worn a good coat and a new hat it would have been different.

It was a long tramp from Trafalgar Square to the docks. Jos would have slept outside some house, or under a bridge near Thames Street, if the Squirrel had not insisted on the folly of such conduct. She said, "You *must* 'ave breakfast."

In Trafalgar Square a man often threw a penny over the wall on his way to work; a daughter of Ill Fame sometimes eased her conscience by giving away her pence. These people had known what it is to be famished, and the Squirrel's great eyes appealed to their sympathies.

One evening, while they were sitting on the stone steps that led into the square, a carriage stopped beside them. A gentleman stepped out of it. He went to the parapet, and looked down for a minute.

Then he returned to the carriage, and said,

" It's quite true; they are sleeping here by hundreds."

" I should like to see," said a voice inside the carriage.

" Oh, you cannot do that."

" Yes I can," the voice persisted.

Afterwards, to the great astonishment of Jos and the Squirrel, a girl, wrapt in a long white cloak stepped out of the carriage, and came close to where they stood gaping at her.

" How terrible !" she exclaimed, looking over the parapet.

"Yes, but it cannot be helped," said her companion; "so it is no good to think about it."

"But it is not just, it is not right!" the girl replied passionately. "Something ought to be done. Why should we have all these luxuries while others are starving? Why——"

"My dear child," the gentleman interrupted, "don't you see that we give work by our luxuries? All we eat and drink, all our entertainments put money into the pockets of the working classes. There must be some scum in a large place like London."

"I do *not* see," the girl said, turning round to look at him. "I wish I had courage to give up all this luxury and laziness; I am so wrapt in wealth that nothing real ever seems to come near me. Yet I know that thousands of people are starving, men and women I could help if I cut myself off from fashion and prejudice. You need not laugh," she continued, seeing a quiet smile playing upon the face of her companion. "I am in earnest. Shall I always bury my conscience?"

"My dear child," the gentleman said, "ever since you read those Socialist books you have talked this absurd nonsense."

The girl made no reply.

"Suppose you did become a Socialist," the gentleman continued; "how could you endure the ostracism of your friends and acquaintances? Besides, what good could you do? The wisest men cannot solve this unemployed problem; and is it likely that a delicate girl like yourself can make any difference?"

Still the girl was silent.

The gentleman spoke again, this time in a very low voice.

"Look here, little sister. If you become a Socialist you will bring disgrace upon us."

Then they went back to the carriage, and drove towards the West End, leaving Jos and the Squirrel very much astonished.

A few nights later orders came to clear the square of vagrants. It was a nuisance for the public to see so much misery. The outcasts must hide away in prisons or workhouses. So much scum was dangerous.

"Pass on, pass on!" said the policemen to vagrants, who had been foolish enough to think that the square belonged to the public.

It was useless to rebel against the huge constables; so they took refuge on the steps of St. Martin's Church, under archways, and on the Embankment. All through one night a little band of fifty men and women walked up and down, outside the square, followed by two enormous policemen.

" We're a desperate lot," said a small, sickly-looking individual. " You'd best not anger us."

The policemen smiled at his impotence.

" Where shall we go ? " said the Squirrel to Jos.

" I'm going," said Jos, " to the workhouse."

CHAPTER XIV.

THE CASUAL WARD OF A WORKHOUSE.

THE following evening, at half-past six o'clock, he went to a casual ward not far from Westminster.

Fifty men stood there already, and a few women ; not in a group, but in a long line that stretched down the street. They were Englishmen, although paupers and vagrants ; so they preferred to represent separate units. Perhaps they did not care to show their small bags, and the bundles that contained all they had left, or to let the others see their hopelessness. One man tried to make a joke. Another sang—

> " What will become of us
>   If things go on this way,
>   If honest working-men
>   Are starving day by day ? "

A third whistled " Starving on the Queen's

Highway," and made grim jests about the Jubilee business.

At last the door opened, and a voice said,

" Come in, twelve of you.   The rest stop outside.   I'm nearly full up."

They passed into a large room, and sat down there on seats to wait.   One by one the master called them to his desk.   Last of all Jos was sent for.

" What is your name ? "

" Joseph Coney."

" How old are you ? "

" Twenty-six."

" What is your parish ? "

" Elmsworth."

" Is that near Old Windsor ? "

"Yes."

"When did you leave Elmsworth?"

" A year ago, all but a few weeks."

'' Why did you come to London ? "

" Work got slack, and I got sacked."

" What's your trade ? "

" I'm a carpenter."

" Have you been employed as a carpenter in London ? ''

" No."

" What have you done then ? "

" I've been at the docks this six months."

" Where did you sleep last night ? "

" On the Embankment."

" Have you been in a casual ward before ? "

" No, never."

" Where are you going when you leave this?"

" I don't know," said Jos, in a voice that was utterly hopeless.

The master entered all these items of interest in his book. Then he asked,

" Have you anything to give me? "

" What do you mean ? "

" Have you a bundle, or anything? You will get it back the day after to-morrow ; but you must not carry anything into your cell."

The young man gave a bitter laugh, and silently showed his empty pockets.

Afterwards he had a bath. He was then taken into a cell that measured eight feet by four feet, at the end of which was a small dark hole called the stone-pit.

The cell was lighted by a jet of gas, and the first thing he saw there was an inscription, written in large uncouth letters on the white-washed wall opposite the entrance.

"I've served my Queen and my country for fifteen years, and this is what I've come to."

He knew who had written it. The writer was the man who had torn up the colonel's letter of recommendation in the public-house; the one who had spoken of whizzing bullets, illness, and thirst in Egypt, to whom the dockman had been merciless because he happened to have a character.

Jos sat down on the low bedstead, and looked at the cell. It had no furniture whatsoever, except the mattress and the rug on which he was sitting. An icy wind swept through the stone pit, so he went to see if a door would shut off the draught. But no door was there, only a large iron window, with bars across, through which flints must be thrown, when broken, into a yard beneath. The wind blew in gusts through the iron bars, and he shivered, for the warm bath made him feel the cold air creeping about his chilly limbs, under his clothes, through his skin to his flesh.

Large blocks of granite lay in the stone pit, also a hammer. There was no seat, and the floor of the place dipped in the middle,

so it was difficult to stand upright. He had
never broken stones in his life. At home
he had seen men stone-breaking. As a child
he had watched flints cracked. Those men
had been provided with strong gloves and
spectacles. In this place a hammer was
thought sufficient.

"You needn't begin till morning," said
the overseer. "Here's your supper. Be
quick. The gas will be turned out in a few
minutes."

So saying, he placed on the floor by the
bed a small tin full of gruel, and a small bit
of bread. (The whole provision could have
been put into a teacup.)

Jos sat down to eat his pauper fare; and
while eating he read again the words of the
soldier:—

"I've served my Queen and my country for
fifteen years, and this is what I've come to."

The gas was suddenly extinguished.

He got under the rug on the bed, and lay
there shivering, half-famished.

Two days and three nights he stayed in that
place, for he could not crack the granite. It
required a knack.

The overseer said, " It's wonderful how stupid some of you fellows are at it. We've got a little hunchback in, and he does it like clockwork ; he squats down close to the floor, and his hammer goes click, click, click, till he's finished. Next time you come here we'll put you to pick oakum ; but we can't let you out till you've cracked that granite."

" Show me the knack," said Jos, whose back ached.

The overseer said, " None of your rubbish."

After he went away Jos thought of the soldier who had written that bitter reproach on the cell wall, who had been sacked at the docks because the men were jealous. He said to himself,

" I'd never have got on there if I'd had a character."

The hours and days passed by slowly.

Three times a day he received his rations of gruel and bread. At night he stopped work when the gas was extinguished ; the rest of the time he stood, or sat, in the stone-pit, trying to find the knack. The stones would not split up small enough to pass through the iron grating ; they either shivered into atoms, or lay on the ground in oblong knobs that no hammer would crack. The stone pit sloped into a hole in the middle, so he found it difficult not to slip when standing up, and impossible to throw stones through the grating when sitting down. Besides, the place was dark, and the damp cold air there made him shiver. A nasty hacking cough had taken possession of him ever since the night of that dream in Trafalgar Square, and his head ached more than it had ever done after any fit of drinking. Again and again he stopped work, for a sharp pain in his side made the hammer fall on the ground as if his hand were palsied.

At last a small bit of granite flew up into his eye, and he walked about the cell in an agony of pain, quite unable to do any more stone breaking.

They let him out the next morning, although the work was not finished, for his eye was blood-shot, and the upper lid had fallen over it. The master tied an old pocket-handkerchief across his forehead, and said,

" Don't come back here within the month. If you do, you'll be kept in twice the time, remember ; but if you come, we'll put you to pick oakum ; you're not good for anything else. It's either your stupidity or your laziness. If a little hunchback can crack granite, a man of your size can do it."

" It's all the knack," said Jos, " it's not laziness."

" That's what the soldier said who was in your cell before you went in," the master said, testily; " he's been scribbling on the wall, I hear. We'll have to get the place whitewashed ; I'll apply for orders to have the men searched. I can't be bothered with so much whitewashing ; and it's just no good to make them empty their pockets."

All the time he lived afterwards Jos never forgot his sensations when the door of the casual ward closed after him that morning. To be once more his own master, after days and nights in that dark, cold place, was in itself happiness. The sun was shining for *him*, the world was *his*, the streets and the sky were *his* property.

He hurried off to Charing Cross, knowing that he would find the Squirrel there. The thought of the little thing filled him for the first time with tenderness. She had been very

good to him. Without her what would he
have done? He must have gone to the workhouse or to prison.

Directly he turned the corner of Trafalgar
Square he saw her quaint figure. He went
softly to the place where she stood selling
flowers, and laid his hand on her basket.

"Oh, Jos!" she said. Then she gave a great
gulp, and stood silent.

He could not interpret her silence; but if
any student of human nature had seen the pale
face, the colourless lips, and the great eyes
with pupils that almost touched their iris, that
student would have known all she was suffering. The triangular shawl and the dirty pinafore
moved quickly up and down, for the heart was
palpitating underneath them, at a rate that
meant real physical suffering. The blood had
left her head, and died out of her cheeks; she
was giddy and faint, unable to say more than
"Oh, Jos!" as though the world held no one
else; and indeed, for her, life without Jos had
become a chaos.

At last she said, "You must 'ave breakfast."

Then she quickly recovered herself, and
asked anxiously what he had done to his eye,

why it was tied up with a pocket-handkerchief?
She made him walk with her to a fountain in
Trafalgar Square, and bathe it with cold water.
It was quite covered now by the swollen
eyelid; but he said that it did not hurt much,
so it was tied up again as before, and they
went to Lockhart's shop, where they "'ad"
breakfast.

Perhaps they made a common-place picture,
sitting by a dirty table, eating mashed potatoes
and sausages; but many an artist would have
brought out his sketch-book had he been in
Lockhart's shop that morning, for the Squirrel's
face looked strangely pathetic, and by her
side was a basket full of autumn roses and
mignonette, close to which sat Jos enjoying
his breakfast.

People came and went, but the two took no
notice. At last every morsel of food had
vanished, the cups of coffee had been emptied,
and turned upside down in East End fashion.

Then the Squirrel asked,

"Why didn't you come out yesterday morning?"

Jos told her how difficult he had found it to
break the granite.

"I'll never go in there any more," he said, "not if I'm starving."

"I've got money," the Squirrel said eagerly. "I stood about that place all day yesterday, but I said to myself, 'When 'e comes out 'e'll want breakfast;' so I went to market this morning, though I did think as I'd never see you again, Jos, and if you'd not come back I'd ——" She stopped.

"You'd what?"

"I'd 'ave drowned myself."

She said this in such a low voice that he did not hear the sentence.

"You'd what?" he repeated.

She made no reply, but took up the basket of flowers, and went back to Trafalgar Square, followed by the young carpenter.

After that he sank yet another step downwards. He could not get work at the docks with a bad eye; no contractor would take him on until he could see again, and for days he was obliged to wear that pocket-handkerchief. He became a corner-man; and stood outside Charing Cross station, touching his hat to ladies who carried parcels, and gentlemen who wanted a hansom.

"Pass on, pass on!" said a policeman.

He lived on the money made by the Squirrel;
and would have starved, if the public had not
bought her roses and mignonette. There was
something in the Squirrel's face that made
people stop by her basket. Her pocket was
never empty, and sometimes she piled up pence
and halfpence into shillings on the pavement.
Jos could not understand how she made so·
much money; but he slowly grew to think it
convenient, and forgot the day when her sixpence was spent in "direa mixture" instead of
breakfast. Sometimes he went into a public-
house; but generally he walked up and down
in front of Charing Cross station, waiting for a
job, with his hands in his pockets.

"Pass on, pass on!" said a policeman.

"I wouldn't speak to a dog as you speak to
me, mister," he said once. "I'm doing no
mischief."

"Pass on, pass on!" said the policeman.

At that time the unemployed were agitating
in Trafalgar Square, and the constables had
lost their patience. What did these men mean
by coming there to say they were hungry?
Why did they force the sight of their misery
upon the public?

"Let's see what they're about," the Squirrel said one day to Jos. "There's a man on the steps I used to know once, a carpenter like you. I thought he'd gone to the work'us."

They elbowed their way in among the crowd, and stood close beneath the steps among a number of working-men, loafers, and corner-men. Not a woman was there, except the little flower-girl, but the men made way for her basket, as she pushed through to hear what the unemployed had to say about being " 'ungry." Jos followed her, with his hands in his pockets. His eye was still bound up with the pocket-handkerchief.

"I've come down 'ere," the speaker was saying when they reached the steps, "on account of all I've read in the papers. Now I don't pay much attention to 'em, for I know they're written by folks as never 'ad a wife ill from want of food, and children starving. If I stood 'ere, and told you 'ow folks live up in Jupiter, you'd say, ' None of your rubbish.' It's just so with the folks as write in the papers, the chaps in Parliament, and the upper classes. They don't know what they're talking about. When I 'ear 'em talk, and read the stuff they write, I says to

myself, 'None of your rubbish.' Now the
papers say no respectable men have been at
these ere demonstrations, nothing but roughs
and idle chaps what wouldn't work if they got
the chance. One chap tells us 'ow 'e set three
men to work for 'im, and 'ow they went off to
a public-'ouse. Another chap says he sent a
shoulder of mutton to a family what said they
were starving, and they asked for onion sauce
to give it a relish. Says I to myself, 'None of
your rubbish.' Now becos the papers tell lies
like this, I've come down 'ere, mates, in my
dinner hour, to show 'em that I'm a legitimate
British labourer, like thousands of men who're
now tramping the streets with empty pockets.
I know, though I've got work to-day, I may be
sacked to-morrow morning, and then I'll have
nothing to do but tramp the streets, or go to
the work'us.

"Look 'ere," he continued, bringing forward
a workman's basket, and producing a hammer,
"is *this* a legitimate workman's tool, or isn't
it ? "

"Yes, yes !" cried a hundred men, laughing.

"Is *this* a legitimate workman's tool ? " he

asked, holding up a screw, "and *this*, and *this*, and *this* ?"

So saying, he showed them the contents of his basket, and held up last of all the tin flask which no British labourer thinks superfluous.

"Yes, yes!" cried his audience.

"Well, mates, six months ago I nearly as possible 'ad to give up and go to the work'us. I couldn't get a job at no price ; and all I 'ad to live on was the money my missus made with 'er machine, dressmaking. Day after day I went to places I saw written about in the papers, and every night I went back to the missus with not a penny in my pocket. She 'ad 'er machine before we were married, and I thought, what with 'er and me, we'd be able to keep a family. But the children came fast,—if the Lord's given me a fruitful vine, I'm not the one to blame 'Im,—and I fell out of work just when the money was wanted most, when another little 'un was coming. My missus got too ill to work the machine, and we were nigh starving. Last of all she says to me, 'You must pawn the machine, Jack. It makes me so bad to 'ear the children cry in their sleep, I can't put up with it.'

"I took the machine to the pawn-shop, and

I'll never forget the look my missus gave me when I came back 'ome again. If I'd not got a job soon after that, I'd 'ave gone on tramp, for I knew my missus and the children would do better without me, they'd 'ave to go into the work'us.

" Now, thank God, I'm in work again, and if I don't get sacked for coming down 'ere this morning, I'll stay where I am, for though the pay's little enough, it comes every week into my pocket. But I says to myself, when I read those lies in the papers, I'll just go to the square, and show 'em I'm a legitimate British labourer."

CHAPTER XV.

THE RIOTS.

AT that time they slept in the doss-house. But they went to Trafalgar Square every morning. The Squirrel found a good market there for her flowers, and Jos always hoped to have a job given him while hanging about outside Charing Cross station. Sometimes he joined the crowd in the square. Once he followed a procession to Hyde Park.

So it went on until Bloody Sunday. That day the Squirrel stood by the post-office, as she had done for weeks, selling roses nipped by night frosts, and autumn violets. Beside her was Jos, with his hands in his pockets.

The church bells rang as usual at eleven o'clock, and the square was quiet. But soon afterwards policemen began to arrive there in hundreds and thousands. Constables picketed their horses at right angles with Nelson's monument.

"What's up?" Jos asked a loafer who had stopped to look at the flowers in the Squirrel's basket.

"Riots."

"Will there be any fighting?"

"Can't tell," answered the loafer. "The police has orders to keep the square empty, and a lot of chaps say they're goin' to get in to hold a meetin'. You'd best carry your basket to Regent Street, miss," he added, turning to the Squirrel. "If you stay here, maybe you'll be run in, anyhow you'll sell nothin'."

"What'll you do?" asked the Squirrel, looking at Jos.

"I'll stay, and see the fun," said Joseph Coney.

"Then I'll not go away," said the Squirrel. "Hark! There's music."

By that time policemen had formed a cordon about the square, two and three deep. Five thousand of the force stood ready to receive the Radicals and Socialists, who had declared their intention of holding a meeting under Nelson's monument, in order to show that the square belonged to the public. At the windows of the clubs, hotels, and houses that overlooked the place, stood crowds of sight-seers, men and women who wanted to have a bird's-eye view of an agitation that had been going on for weeks, an agitation about to reach its climax. Was it true that the agitators were "'ungry," or was it false? Did the genuine unemployed come to these daily demonstra-tions, or were the demonstrators loafers who would not work, vagrants who wanted to play on the sympathies of the public, scum that must be allowed to die like dogs in the streets by order of Political Economists?

Jos and the Squirrel stared up at these people, and while they were staring two young men from the West End stopped by the post-office. These men talked to one another in the drawling way, that has been in vogue among such people for half a century.

"'Pon my honour, I can't see why Salisbury lets things go on like this," said one of them, looking at the cordon of policemen through his eye-glass. "The unemployed are an awful nuisance. Why doesn't Salisbury let them make another Thames tunnel?"

"Ah! Yes," said his companion, "they might do that, and fill it up again."

"'Pon my honour, I'll write to the *Morning Post*, and propose it."

"No, don't. I'll tell Bob Cecil. Awful clever fellow Bob Cecil. Knows everything."

They walked on.

It is a great misfortune that this brilliant suggestion has been lost to the public!

The roads about the square now became filled with men and women, who pressed in from all sides, and moved towards the cordon of policemen.

"Pass on, pass on!" said the mounted constables, riding slowly about amongst the crowd.

The crowd kept moving, for it only wanted to see the fun, not to take part in any demonstration. But presently one of the Radical clubs came up a side street, and the policemen received orders to close on it. Banners were seized and broken, a drum was smashed, musical instruments were thrown on the ground and trampled under foot. The club was driven back. But only for a minute. A low angry hiss was heard amongst the men, and they pressed on again, fighting their way with sticks and fists, while the bâtons of the policemen returned their blows with interest. The police hit right and left. Their blood was up. They had been kept on duty day and night for the last few weeks, and this was their first real chance of letting the unemployed know what it is to be overworked. The club fell back once more, hissing.

Then " on there came a hungry people," north, south, east, and west of the square, with music and banners. The police grew furious. They fell upon one club after another, led by the mounted constables ; and news came that fighting was going on at Westminster, in Holborn, along Piccadilly, and up the side streets that led to the place Sir Charles Warren had closed to the public.

The crowd of sightseers became filled in with angry processionists, whose anger spread in all directions, when a mounted constable knocked over a man, and the horse trod upon him, when the bâtons of the policemen fell on the heads of men and breasts of women, when man after man, and woman after woman was thrown down and trampled upon. Denser and denser grew the crowd about the square. Louder and louder became the hisses. Nearer and nearer the people pressed on to the cordon of policemen that shut them off from the place which belongs to the public.

The Squirrel and Jos were sucked into the mob, and could not get out again. They felt it moving like one man towards the square, and felt it surge back, hissing. The Squirrel's face was pale as death. But she liked the movement. She crept close to Jos, forgetting her flower-basket that had been torn away by the mob. Her little heart beat fast. She hissed loudly, not knowing why, but feeling the noise a relief in her intense excitement. Then some one said,

" The soldiers are coming ! "

The whole scene was like a nightmare, after reading a chapter of Carlyle's " French Revolution."

But the hisses were real enough, for they meant starvation and hopelessness. And since Justice rules the universe, those hisses rise up into the ears of the Lord God of Sabaoth.

The drama was not without a comic element ; for certain men and women went to the cordon of policemen, asking to be arrested ; and the huge constables, drawing themselves up to their full height, said,

" We cannot do it unless you assault us."

Success is never absurd. Failure is often ridiculous. This thing is certain—if more people had followed the example of those men and women, if it had *really* been a Bloody Sunday, that labour programme which is looming in the distance would now be before Parliament ; Lord Salisbury and his party would ere this have vanished into nothingness.

Then what would become of foreign politics ?

For on the Continent are rumours of wars. Men's hearts are failing them for the days that must shortly come upon us. The pillars of an empire that has kept Europe stable for years are tottering ; and when they fall, the whole weight of the structure must rest on the shoulders of a man who, at the most, knows the right position for an epaulet. France is breathing hatred, and panting to shed the last drop of her blood in vengeance. The northern bear lies with a paw on Roumania, and his eyes fixed on the sick man we have so long bolstered up for the peace of Europe. When the war begins

we shall be dragged into it, unless by that time
we have "scuttled" out of Egypt.

"The soldiers are coming!" cried the
Squirrel quivering with excitement. "Oh, Jos!
will they shoot us?"

It seemed as if the shades of the Stuarts
had returned, after centuries spent in Latin
Prayer-books, for mounted-guards trotted slowly
into the square, headed by a magistrate who
had come to read the Riot Act.

Then some one said, "They've broken the
back of the riot," for, as the mounted-guards
advanced, the hisses grew less, and a faint
cheer was heard near the National Gallery
where the foot-guards had halted.

It was almost dark, but coloured lights
showed a thin, glittering line of steel advanc-
ing towards the cordon of policemen. Five
minutes later soldiers formed a frieze about the
square, and stood with fixed bayonets.

The people stopped hissing to watch these
military manœuvres, and crowded on to the
pavement, to make way for the horses and the
grave men who sat on them, with plumes
nodding. Then the hissing began again, and
the policemen who had been set free by the

foot-guards, rushed on the men and women with bâtons and fists, the mounted constables charged with double fury, because they felt that the soldiers were watching their movements.

In one of those ugly rushes in which so many people were injured, Jos was thrown against a policeman by some men, who were struggling to escape from the wheels of an omnibus. With a blow the policeman knocked him down on the ground, muttering,

"Get up, or I'll run you in, you d— rascal."

They had been running men in all the afternoon, and had just taken off an M.P. to prison ; so this young man, with his eye bound up by a pocket-handkerchief, was poor game one would think. But as he struggled to his feet, and a cry of "Shame, shame!" was heard amongst the crowd, two policemen seized him, and he was dragged away, almost unconscious of what was taking place, to Bow Street. "Shame, shame!" cried the men and women. "Let him alone!" "What's he done?" "I saw you knock him down, and kick him!" The policemen took no notice, but hurried him along through the mob to the police station, where he was placed in the dock, and charged with assaulting one of Her Majesty's servants.

Then they locked him up in a cell with three men, who had been run in the previous day for drinking. That place needs a Zola to do it justice. There was one long seat in it, on which sat a besotted drunkard; and when Jos was led in the gaoler stumbled over a drunken man who lay on the floor, sick as a dog, from drinking.

" You're in good company," said the gaoler. " There's an M.P. going to be locked up. Orders have come that bail's not to be taken for him on no account. He'll have the cell next to you, I think."

" Have you any money to buy supper ? " he asked. " None ? Then you'll get some coffee and bread, when we've time to send for it. I'll bring you a mattress."

He went away, leaving Jos to think of all that had taken place, to wonder in what way, and by whom, Her Majesty's servant had been " assaulted."

" I did nothing to him," said Jos. " What do they mean by running me in like this ? "

There is in every Englishman a strong prejudice against injustice, and even a weak young man like Joseph Coney, knew what it meant to be run in for nothing.

What had he done? How had he assaulted the policeman?

So he asked himself all through that long dark night, while he lay among these dregs of the populace, and he became more and more hopeless. Why not steal? Why not drink? The fumes of the putrid cell mounted up with the hot air to the ceiling and could not escape; the iron door was bolted. Sleep would not come to him; so he lay awake hour after hour, listening to those drunken men, who were snoring.

It was eleven o'clock the next morning before his trial took place. He had some coffee and bread for breakfast. Afterwards he waited in a room, among other prisoners until some one said, "You next."

Then he followed a policeman into court, and stood in the dock, before the magistrate. The place was crowded. People had come to see the M.P. and the well-known Socialist who had been run in for assaulting policemen.

"When I was in Trafalgar Square, your

Worship," began No. — A.R. Then he paused, and looked at the prisoner.

Jos stood with his head bent down, and his eyes fixed on the boards below the dock. The expression of his face was utterly hopeless.

No. — A.R. continued his evidence, and pointed to a scratch on his cheek which had (so he said) been inflicted by the prisoner on the way to Bow Street.

"Now what have you got to say to this?" the magistrate asked Jos.

"It's false!" said Jos, without looking up. "It's false!"

"Is there any witness for the prisoner?" inquired the magistrate.

"Yes," said a voice behind the seats close to the principal entrance. Then the Squirrel stepped into the witness-box.

"The evidence that you give to the court shall be the truth, the whole truth, and nothing but the truth. So help me God."

The Squirrel kissed the sacred book, and the court became so quiet that one might have heard a pin drop.

She did not wait to be questioned, but began to speak at once. Her great eyes flashed down at No. — A.R. who sat among a dozen policemen on the front bench; and shaking her fist, she said, in a voice choked by anger, full of passionate reproach,

"You knocked him down, you did! You knocked him down, and he wasn't doing nothing. You're a bad man, you're a d— liar, you're the greatest liar that's ever lived; you tried to kill him, and I thought he was dead. Oh, Jos, they'll lock you up, and I'll never see you again, and you haven't done nothing."

Then she laid her head on the ledge in front of the witness-box, and covered her face with her dirty pinafore. The court could hear her sobbing.

"What does she say?" inquired the old magistrate, putting his hand to his ear, for he is very deaf.

"She says No. — A.R. is a d— liar, your worship."

The prisoner was ordered to pay 2s. 6d., or to suffer four days' imprisonment.

Jos left the court with the gaoler. The Squirrel trotted behind them. When they reached the place where the fines are paid, she produced a dirty pocket-handkerchief. She counted two shillings in coppers on the desk, and then she placed on them a silver sixpence. A jackdaw stood near the fine book; and he gave the Squirrel a quizzical look when she produced the silver sixpence, as much as to ask,

"Where did you get that money?"

The Squirrel looked at him; then she said,

"If I *did* steal it, Jack, it's none of your business."

She left the place with Jos. The young man was silent, until they came to a gin-shop; then he stopped.

"Have you got any money?" he asked.

"Oh, Jos!" she said, "come home with me; don't go into that place."

"Have you got any money?" he asked again.

She slowly untied the dirty pocket-handkerchief. Afterwards she turned away. She had given him her last penny.

CHAPTER XVI.

UNCLE COHEN ON THE SITUATION.

THE evening of that same day, the door of Uncle Cohen's little shop was pushed open, and Polly went in. She seated herself opposite a long looking-glass, took off her hat, and began slowly to unplait her hair. When the yellow stuff fell over her shoulders, she put her elbows on the marble slab in front of her, rested her head on her hands, and looked into the glass. " I'm sure William Ford's going to ask me to marry him," sighed Polly. " What a pity it is Jos isn't a Methodist ! "

" Who're you talking to ? " asked the Jew, coming into the shop.

" Myself," answered Polly. " I've just come from class ; I thought I'd look in, and get my hair cut."

The Jew brought out a large white sheet which he put round her. Then he went to a

cupboard, and chose two of his best brushes.
Afterwards he took a comb, and with it he
divided the hair in the centre; he passed the
yellow stuff tenderly through his fingers. If a
princess had come there, he would not have
treated the royal head with so much reverence,
have done his work with such care, have
lingered so long over his hair-dressing.

"Whose head's that?" asked Polly, looking
up at Mr. Gladstone's picture. "I've often
been here before, but I never thought to ask;
whose head is it?"

"Mr. Gladstone's," said the Jew.

"Who's he?" inquired Polly.

"He's a genius," answered Uncle Cohen.
"Leastways the papers say so lately."

"What's a genius?" asked Polly.

"My dear, I can't tell you," said Uncle
Cohen. "But I know that's what the papers
call him, besides the Grand Old Man, and
a lot of names what have no meaning."

"Stop brushing," said Polly, "I want the
ends cut."

The Jew brought a pair of scissors out of
his pocket, but then hesitated.

"It's a sin to cut it," he said.

"Singe it," said Polly.

"Singe it!" exclaimed Uncle Cohen. "Singe it!"

"Well, be quick," Polly said, "I must be going home. Don't keep me waiting."

The shop was very small. It had no furniture but the two large chairs in front of the looking-glasses. One door opened into the street, the other into a room where the Jew slept, cooked, and performed all his domestic and business operations. Into that room no one ever penetrated but himself. No one had been inside it since the day he arrived there first, and no one would go in until the Death Watch sat down beside his bed to say when body and spirit parted. (Uncle Cohen would have a Death Watch although he called himself a sceptic.) He ran the comb through Polly's hair, but when the scissors touched it he soon stopped. He put the scissors back in his pocket, and began to brush the hair softly, with long even strokes, from the parting downwards. Then he plaited it.

"It's done now," said Polly, throwing off the sheet. "It looks very nice, Uncle Cohen."

She spoke in rather a tired voice, and as

the Jew took the sheet away he noticed that she looked pale, as though she had been crying.

"What is it, little woman?" he asked tenderly. "What's the matter?"

"I can't tell you," said Polly, shaking her head. "You wouldn't understand if I did. Oh, Uncle Cohen," she continued, getting up and kissing him, "I wish I was an old man like you, with my life over and done with, not a girl like myself."

Nice for the Jew, was it not?

He made no answer. Polly put on her hat, wished him good-night, and, went away. When the door had closed after her he picked up the ends of hair that had fallen on the floor; he put them into a drawer, in which he had more than one reminiscence of Polly, where a little white sock, a broken teacup, and a faded geranium lay already. He stored the yellow hair like gold there. Then he went into his other room, and sat down on the bed, thinking.

That "other room" was even stranger than the shop to look at. The small low bedstead had the Jew's coats stretched across it for a counterpane, and on the pillow lay his night-cap, a knitted thing, half a yard in length, and a few inches in circumference. By the fire was his supper, poodle-soup, that he had made himself. Saucepans full of grease, and pots of hairwash were on a table by the fire-place; also half-made wigs, plaits of hair, screws for extracting teeth, and specimens of other things which he exhibited in his shop window.

"Well, she'll be marrying one of these days," the Jew said to himself, " marrying some young feller what'll make a drudge of her. Young men don't know how to treat a wife— leastways, not one like Polly.

"It isn't every woman as I'd care to marry. Fact is, till Polly grew up, I said to myself as I didn't want to marry nobody. It was Elwin's wife what set me against marrying. The life she led him! I do believe they hadn't been married a week afore she'd emptied all his cupboards, and turned out all his pockets. Says I to myself, 'If that's what Elwin's got to put up with, what's got a house full of lodgers, and a many rooms for his wife to pry into, whatever would a woman do by me, in but two rooms, where she and me'd have to keep close company ?'

"I did think once as I might chalk a partition. Says I to myself, 'I'll marry, and I'll say to her, "What's mine's over here, and what's yourn's over there ; there's no good, missus, in muddling things together."'

"But bless you, directly my back was turned she'd have skipped across the chalk, the very first time I went out she'd have been ferreting in my things, and turning out my pockets. And to hear Mother Elwin going on about religion ! Why, when I hear her I can't help picturing of the Almighty like an Aunt Sally down on Mile End Waste, with prayers flying at His head like cocoa nuts. To hear her talk one would think she'd shaken hands with Him already !

"She told me last week as she was looking forrard to talking with St. Paul stead of me of a Sunday. Says I to myself, 'St. Paul must be a deal foolisher than the Bible makes him out to be, if he's taken in by you, old lady.' Make me a Christian ! Me ? Thank you. What with their big says and little does, I'd rather be a Jew.

"Now it's like a breath of fresh air to go and hear Bradlaugh after listening to Mother Elwin's jaw about religion. He's a Jew, says I. He believes in a God, does Charley, but not a god as people can make for themselves; a real God, the God of Abraham, Isaac, and Jacob, what all sensible people believe in. I'll take my Davy, that I will, Charley hasn't made as many sceptics as Christians has done with their queer religion! But it's different with Polly. I'd no more laugh at her now than I'd have done when she nursed her doll on my knee as a baby. To please her I'd go to synagogue, though I can't say as I care to hear them sing-songing, and wear a white napkin. To please Polly, I declare I'd go to chapel.

"But she'd no more look at me than Father Christmas. She'll marry some young feller what'll make a drudge of her."

The Jew got off his bed, and emptied the poodle-soup into a basin. It was almost dried up, and it did not tempt his appetite. He seated himself by the table covered with wigs, brushes, and other things, and there he sat, staring at his supper. About his heart was a feeling old bachelors are supposed to know nothing about, a feeling called "heartache." The Jew felt just then tired of everything. He thought that he would not be sorry when the Death Watch came into his place, and he waited for that kiss of the God of Abraham, Isaac, and Jacob, which Jews call Death.

Presently he heard the door-bell ringing. He went into his shop, where stood a Je wess, who had come to have her hair shaved off for the West End market. She stepped quietly into the seat Polly had vacated half an hour before. The Jew put the same sheet round her. Then he went to a drawer to fetch a razor. As he bent down his head a tear fell there; and for days afterwards there was a spot of rust among the razors and stropes, a speck that was at last rubbed away on the chin of a man who came into the shop, and said, "I want shaving."

CHAPTER XVII.

SHE JILTS HIM.

POLLY walked slowly towards home after she left the Jew's shop, thinking, as she went, of the class meeting, and saying to herself,—

"What a pity it is Jos isn't a Methodist!" For weeks and months she had not seen him.

Mrs. Elwin sometimes said in a mysterious way,—

"He's come to no good, Polly. If he'd got work, he'd have been here long before this."

Polly knew that he had not left London, for every week she received a letter from him. But he gave no address; and the answers, which she sent to the place where he had gone, with two boxes, after he left Mrs. Elwin's house, had all come back again, "On Her Majesty's service."

"Perhaps," said Mrs. Elwin, "he's in the workhouse."

The Wesleyans had lately opened a Mission Hall for the poorer classes near Ratcliffe Highway. "Middling folks," like Mrs. Elwin and her daughter, had poured out tea there; and after the cups and saucers had been cleared away, Mr. Meek and Mr. Stry had given addresses to the assembled audience. Last of all, William Ford had spoken a few words on the following subject,

"Can a man be saved if he is not a Methodist?"

Tears had rolled down Mrs. Elwin's cheeks while the class-leader spoke of the narrow path trodden by Methodists; and she had whispered to her daughter,—

"Oh, Polly! To think you might marry such a godly young man, with a settled income."

The pretty Methodist was thinking of all this as she turned the corner of Commercial Street. There she suddenly stopped, for she saw coming towards her the very person she did not wish to meet, namely, Joseph Coney, who was on his way to the doss-house. He was sauntering carelessly along with his hands in his pockets. Why should he hurry? Nothing could be done that day. To-morrow he would try to get a job at the docks, and if work was not to be had there, he would go on to Charing Cross station. He stood quite still when he caught sight of the pretty Methodist. Every trace of colour left his pale face for a minute. Then he walked quickly up to her, and said,—

" Polly ! "

" Jos ! "

They looked at one another in silence.

He was conscious of his untidy appearance ; for the days when he had arrived at Mrs. Elwin's house with *two* boxes had not faded from his memory, although they belonged to the dim past, and between him and them lay a weary time of misery and disappointment. He had just come out of prison. What would Polly say if she knew that he had spent last night at Bow Street ?

The girl's face expressed first astonishment, then disgust. This man in ragged clothes and battered hat, whose boots had holes in them, whose eye was bound up with a dirty pocket-handkerchief, who could he be ? Was he really

Joseph Coney? She shrank away as he approached, and drew nearer and nearer to the edge of the pavement.

"Well, Polly," he said, in rather a husky voice, "you've not seen me this long while. You might say something."

"You sent back my letters," began Polly, slowly.

"I didn't."

"Some one did then."

"It wasn't me, Polly."

"You haven't been to see me; and mother says——"

"Come, Polly," he said, "none of this rubbish."

She paused for a minute. Then she continued in a low voice,—

"Mother says I've no right to marry a man what isn't a Methodist."

"Methodists be hanged!" he answered fiercely. "What does your mother mean by talking of Methodists?"

"Oh, Jos," said Polly, "to hear you talk, one would say you was an atheist."

He laughed, then he came closer to her, and said,—

"Look here, Polly, I know your mother hates me. Let's do something. Let's emigrate. You promised to marry me or nobody. The last thing you said to me was, 'Things will come right yet, Jos.'"

The girl drew back. And then being unable to make any more excuses, feeling that she must put an end to it, she blurted out the truth.

"I'm not going to marry you, Joseph Coney; I'm going to marry a godly young man with a settled income."

He caught hold of her wrist, and looked at her for half a minute. Then he said,—

"You little hypocrite!"

Afterwards he turned away, and walked towards the doss-house. As he went, she could hear him laughing, and saying to himself, "The little hypocrite!"

She stood staring after him for some time, unable to believe that this was the end of their friendship. Her wish was accomplished. He had gone away. But the end had come so unexpectedly, in so few minutes, that the present seemed a blank, without any past, without any future that seemed to fit in with it. For instead of leaving her on a pedestal of righteousness,

Jos had rudely kicked the stool of self-respect from beneath her feet. He had called her a little hypocrite.

She walked on home, trying as she went to soothe her conscience. She called Jos an atheist (to do her justice, she scarcely knew what that term of opprobrium meant; very few people do, who use it), and said to herself,—

"It could have been nothing but misery to marry a man what isn't a Methodist."

She even went so far as to think of the children that might have been cursed by a father whose opinions were so pernicious (her mother had spoken to her on the subject); but then she believed in an Omnipotent Being Who can make black white, and she was aware that if there is a hell for atheists, she ought to have saved Jos from falling into it.

Mary Anne opened the door for her, and she hurried upstairs to her bedroom. There she tried to wash away the black finger-marks that Jos had left on her wrist; they seemed to say, "You little hypocrite!" Having lived for many years on a pedestal of righteousness, it was not pleasant to feel like this. She sought among all her mental salves for something to soothe

her conscience.   Still she heard the words,
"You little hypocrite!"

It grew late, but she did not go downstairs
to supper.   She sat by the table trying to make
excuses for herself.   At last she was cheered
by the thought that, although Jos might be
unhappy for a time, he would soon get over his
disappointment.   Then she would be very kind
to him.   She would ask him to dinner every
Sunday (and he would come, of course!), just
as Uncle Cohen came to her mother's house.
He *must* see, by-and-by, that she could not
have married a man "out of work," a man "what
wasn't a Methodist."

Presently Mrs. Elwin came upstairs to put
out the gas, and went into the adjoining bedroom.

"Shingles!"   Polly heard her mother say
contemptuously to an Algerian merchant who
lay there ill in bed.   "What's shingles?   You
foreign folks think you're going to die if you've
a thumb ache.   Got it from the sheets!
Rubbish!   Shingles don't come in that way,
man; they're in the constitution.   You got a cold
when you stood your feet in that water yesterday.   Serves you right, shingles does, for your

heathen ways of going on; shingles is in the constitution."

Afterwards, Mrs. Elwin opened the door of Polly's room and asked,

"Why didn't you come downstairs to supper?"

"I didn't want nothing to eat," said the pretty Methodist.

"What's the matter?"

"I've a headache."

"Polly," said Mrs. Elwin, fixing her keen blue eyes on the girl's face, "has William Ford declared hisself?"

"Oh, mother, do leave me alone to-night!" cried Polly. "I've got a headache."

Mrs. Elwin had been a girl herself, so she knew what it all meant. She left the room, saying to herself,

"It's all right; Polly 'll tell me about it at breakfast."

Directly the door was shut Polly went to the chest of drawers, and brought out a box that contained some letters from Joseph Coney. They were written in the large unformed hand of a school-boy; their sentences were like moral precepts, copied from some children's lesson book.   Reading them, she could see that he was very unhappy.   He spelt adversity with a big A ; and said if the Almighty would give him a job, he'd ask no more of Him.   Moreover, she was obliged to confess that Jos was not an atheist ; for the letters expressed an amount of resignation that bordered on hopelessness.

" Poor Jos ! " she said.   Then she put the letters back in the box with William Ford's photograph.

While she was doing this the door was softly opened, and Mary Anne came in.   The little maid servant wore a short dark ulster that showed her bare feet, and her nightdress.   Her hair was rolled up in curl papers, that gave her face a comic appearance ; her eyes were wide open, as though she had had some nightmare.

" Miss Polly ! " she said in a low voice.   " Ho ! Miss Polly, hi've had such a scare, miss."

" Well," said Polly, " what was it ? "

" I saw you laid hout in your coffin.   Ho ! " (Mary Anne began to cry) " Ho, you did make such a beautiful corpse, miss ! "

Polly shuddered.

" Go back to bed," she said.   " It's those

silly stories you read, Mary Anne, that make you talk such rubbish. I'll call mother if you stand there crying. You ought to be ashamed of yourself."

Mary Anne left the room, rubbing her eyes with the sleeve of her ulster. Her bare feet pattered down the steps to the kitchen, where a dip candle flared on a table, among plates and dishes, cups and basins, and cooking utensils that were waiting to be washed up.

On the low bed sat a rat, upright.

"Harrah!" cried Mary Anne, clapping her hands. "Be hoff, you varmint!"

The rat disappeared under the bed, and Mary Anne crept between the blankets.

"Now hi'd be fond of Miss Polly, hi would, hif she'd only let me," said the little maid servant. "It's so lonesome here in the kitchen. That dream made my blood creep. Hi only wanted to see hif she was hall right. She's so huppish!"

Meanwhile Polly undressed, and knelt down to say her prayers as she had done from child-hood. But for some reason or other words halted, sentences seemed to stagnate. She had not been loyal to Jos; worse than that, she had not been loyal to the God of Methodists. Although she had washed her wrist, the red marks on it said, "You little hypocrite!" Whatever salve she might apply later on to her conscience, it said then in an uncompromising voice, "You have told lies, you have broken a promise."

In the adjoining bedroom the Algerian merchant lay snoring, It was hard indeed to be in a house full of Turks, infidels, and heretics, and yet to feel a hypocrite!

"O God!" she began to pray.

But she could not go on.

Where was Joseph Coney? He had looked so pale and thin ; his eye had been bound up with a pocket-handkerchief.

"O God!" she said again.

Then she got into bed, for she found it impossible to go on praying.

The house was very quiet. She could hear the clock in the hall ticking ; and it seemed to say, "You little hypocrite!"

She turned restlessly from side to side. She could not sleep. The clock ticked, "Hypocrite! Hypocrite!"

CHAPTER XVIII.

HIS LAST NIGHT IN LONDON.

JOS walked up the street, saying to himself, " The little hypocrite ! "

He felt stunned ; it took him at least five minutes to realise what had happened. " The little hypocrite ! " he muttered between his teeth. Then he gave the same laugh that had rung round Nelson's monument, and echoed among the pillars of the National Gallery, a month before ; a laugh in which there was not the ghost of merriment, only that bitterness and that contempt which arise from unjust treatment.

Presently he thought of Polly's last sentence, " I'm going to marry a godly young man with a settled income."

He stood still, for a sudden spasm of jealousy seized him.

Until that night he had trusted her too much

to be jealous. Sometimes, when he had heard her speak of the class-leader, the thought had crossed his mind, "I wish I d work in the Mint, where pay's regular, where there's no slack time." But that Polly would jilt him had never entered his head, for he had looked upon her as a superior sort of creature, one who would not tell a lie, or break a promise; besides, her last words to him had been, "Things will come right yet, Jos;" and he had said those words to himself over and over again, during the weary days and months in which he could not find work. Those words had been with him in Trafalgar Square, the casual ward, and the prison cell; he had seemed to see the fair hair, the neat figure, and the modest face of the pretty Methodist, and to hear her say, "I'll marry you, or nobody!" Then he had conjured up a picture of days that must surely come later on, of a time when he would have regular work and good wages.

"There's some mistake," he said to himself. But no, she had told him plainly enough, "I'm not going to marry you, Joseph Coney; I'm going to marry a godly young man with a settled income."

He laughed again, and struck his foot angrily on the pavement. He might have been certain that she would do this, "the little hypocrite!" Why had he let her drift away? He had known perfectly well that her mother hated him, that such a pretty girl must have half-a-dozen men waiting for her. Why had he trusted to those letters? If he had gone to see her the day his clothes were out of the pawn-shop, everything would have been different.

Passers-by took no notice of him. If people paused to interpret the white face and fixed stare of every man or woman who stands like an automaton in the streets, they would not have time to do their own business. A "hurdy-gurdy" played "Oh, what a surprise! Two lovely black eyes!" close beside him. A Toyn-beeite hurried past him, with a bran-new scheme for raising the masses bulging from the pocket of a short black jacket. He could hear the drums of the Whittington boys in the distance. Hundreds of people came and went while he stood there, thinking.

If he had not trusted Polly so much, he said to himself, it would all have been different. But somehow or other she had not seemed to

him quite like other women; she had been
connected in his mind with things at home, with
his mother who lay six feet in the earth, his
one relation.   Now she had jilted him because
he was out of work—she had given him up for
a man with a settled income.

He glanced at his ragged clothes and old
boots for half a minute.   Polly had looked at
him with disgust, she had shrunk away to the
edge of the pavement.   Well, he *did* look like
a tramp, there was no doubt about that; but
it was not his fault.   He had done his best to
get work ever since he had arrived at Mrs.
Elwin's house in tidy clothes, with *two* boxes.
He had not been able to find a job as a
carpenter; but then, if master-carpenters like
Reeson had to go into the workhouse, what
could *he* expect?   He was nothing but a village
artist.

Presently he seemed to see Polly in the
sitting-room, where he had seen her first,
bending over her work.   They had spent many
happy days there together, talking over the
little house in Hackney, to which the butcher
would pay constant visits.   He would never see
her again; she had jilted him; that man William

Ford, would be there; that man would kiss her; that man——

He started, and began to walk towards the class-leader's house, feeling that he would like to wring the godly young man's neck, to do something desperate.

But he was too weak and ill for passion to have much hold on him. He stopped, laughed, and muttered between his teeth, "The little hypocrite!"

Then he turned to look for a public-house, feeling that he would like a glass of spirits. He knew how the gin would soak into his flesh, and deaden his consciousness. "After all," he said to himself, "I'm more to blame than any one else. Why did I trust the little hypocrite?"

So saying, he pushed open the doors of a gin-shop, and went to the bar. Half-a-dozen men and women stood there, drinking. On a narrow wooden bench sat a little Jewess, holding a fowl in her arm, which would by-and-by be killed in Hebrew fashion. (Whitechapel presents many ghastly sights to the public; but none more ghastly than the hen-market.)

The barmaid asked, "What's your order, mister?"

He put his hand into his pocket. Then
he turned sheepishly away, and as he left
the place, he heard the jeers of men, the
laughter of women, and the cackling of the
hen, the feathers of which were being plucked
by the little Jewess. Out in the street damp
air wrapt him round like a blanket; he staggered to a lamp-post (he was not drunk, only
weak and half famished). Close by him was a
penny-gaff, outside which stood men brandish-
ing swords, inviting people to see a skeleton
arm, "a sight every mother ought to witness."
At the present time it pays better to be born
a monstrosity than a man possessed of nothing
but labour force. The former can make £5 a
night by standing still to be stared at; the
latter is a drug in the market. The youth with a
skeleton arm came to the door; he was dressed
à la Buffalo Bill, and balanced a spear on his
chin. He went back to perform other deeds of
prowess; and people flocked in to see "a sight
every mother ought to witness."

Jos walked past the penny-gaff without
looking into it. Men and women jostled
him, but he took no notice of them. He
did not see the old women selling winkles

and pigs' feet; the old men hawking boot laces; the stalls covered with cheap goods and finery; the papers and the advertisements. He felt ill and hopeless. Polly had been the last link he had left with his past life, a past as different from the present time as light is from darkness. Now she had jilted him. It was too late to begin again, he had not strength to struggle against that adversity which he spelt with a big A. He had said over and over again, "If God Almighty will only give me a job I'll ask no more of Him"; and nothing had come of it.

Adversity had driven him to the gin-shop, as it drives men every day who have no work, who are not wanted. He craved for gin. From the day on which the dock-labourer's wife had fetched him "three penn'orth of spirits," a craving for gin had taken possession of him. As the dock-labourer said—"He had fallen to drink as though it had come down from father to son; it was in the constitootion."

Halfway up the Waste he was stopped by the wife of this very same dock-labourer.

"Why, Mr. Coney," she said, "we've not

seen you this long while. What's the matter
with your eye?"

"How's the kid?" asked Jos.

"Nicely, thank you. Come and have supper
with us. My husband will be right down glad
to see you. Do now, Mr. Coney."

Jos shook his head, and walked on. He
passed the People's Palace, and turned to the
right. Then he stopped to look into a room
that held a large bed. On it lay six men, and
beside it was an old Chinese woman filling
pipes with opium. He thought that he would
like to try that narcotic; but he had no money
to pay for a pipe, so he moved away from the
cracked window, and walked into a narrow
alley through which coffins can only be carried
upright. This led into a court, that had half-
a-dozen broken-down houses at the top, and a
low wall at the bottom. Some people, who
had been evicted by the landlord, were sleeping
there under a tent. He looked over the wall
into the canal beneath, and while he was
looking two women brought a sailor out of a
house. One held the sailor's head, the other
carried his feet; they lifted him over the wall,
and let him fall on a parapet.

" Drugged," said Jos to himself.   " I wonder if he'll lie there, or if he'll fall into the river ! "

He left the alley, and passed the house in which lives the East End countess.   This woman has not for twenty years seen daylight. She owns half the street and a large public-house at the corner ; she occupies a dirty place full of cats, donkeys, and parrots.   A pet spaniel of hers one day fell over the wall at the back, and a potman picked it up.   She made that potman master of her public-house, where he drank himself to death.   Her property will one day come to a nephew, who is given to drinking.   She was jilted in her youth, and from that day to this she has never seen day-light.   " If a man 'ad treated me like that," the Squirrel once said to Jos, " I'd just 'ave killed myself."

Jos looked up at the window, and thought for a minute about the vagaries of the East End countess.   Then he walked on.   He passed the place in which turtles are kept for the Lord Mayor's banquets ; and wondered how they like a lingering death, for they have their throats cut early in the morning and die late at night.   At last he came to the river,

and went down to the water's edge among the
hulks and the barges. He could see coloured
lights, and smell seaweed. But it was cold
there, and gusts of wind made him shiver. So
he went back to the main road, where people
bought and sold, talked and quarrelled, where
he did not know a single human being. The
streets swarmed with men, women, and children,
the open doors of the houses showed rooms
teeming with inhabitants ; but he was as lonely
there as in a sepulchre. Had he worn a gold
chain, some one would have robbed him ; had
he been a Jack Tar, some siren would have
beguiled him into a public-house. But he
looked like a tramp, so no one took any notice,
unless he knocked up against a man who swore
at him, or jostled a woman who tried to push
him off the pavement.

He wandered on to the quaint old church.
Just then the belfry bells began ringing. He
stopped to listen. The chimes seemed far
away from the noisy city, like the echoes
of bells he had known long ago, the bells of
his native village. He thought of the churchyard, where his mother lay, that quiet, quiet
place, where the moonlight glinted on the

graves through the dark fir trees. "Silent and Safe" had been written on his mother's tombstone. She had wished it. Now John Datchett the rector, lay, no doubt, close beside her. Jos remembered the day on which he had been to say good-bye at the rectory.

"There's just room for me, Jos, sixteenth rector of this parish," the clergyman had told him, pointing to a list of names in a frame above the fireplace. Then Jos had said to himself, "They say in the village the rector's got a worse complaint than rheumatics." He thought of the tall man with white hair and bending figure, whose calm, patient face had year after year been seen in the village pulpit. The rector had said to him, "Try to get work near home, Jos; don't go to that great Babylon where you have no friend, stop near the village."

Suddenly he said to himself, "I'll go back home again."

No sooner had that idea come into his head than he longed to put it into practice. His mother was dead, so was John Datchett. He did not wish to see the villagers, who would laugh at him for coming back without any money. But the thought of home was a great relief. He was weak and ill. Polly had jilted him. He would get away from this noisy city, where there was no work for him, where he was not wanted. He would go back to his native place, for he felt so ill. "Maybe," he said to himself, "I'm dying."

But he could not go without money. He must have something to eat on the way, even if he tramped the whole journey. Thirty-five miles is not a great distance, but too far for a man to walk with an empty stomach. Then he remembered that his watch was still in the pawn-shop. He had hesitated to sell it, for it was the last thing that his mother had given him. He would take the money for that, he said to himself, and start off home the following morning.

A strange feeling of restfulness took possession of him when he saw his way clear to leave the city. He began to think of the days when he had lived with his mother in a small cottage, and of the village workshop. He had made all things in that place, from coffins to cradles; and he had been proud then of his own cleverness. It was only after he came to London that he found out

"I'm nothing but a village artist." Down there he had been reckoned a clever young man, one above the average in intelligence. Until work got slack in the village, and he was turned away, there was not a more hopeful man than Joseph Coney.

He left the church, and walked on to find a bed, saying to himself, "I'll be off early to-morrow morning." And walking along he thought of "the lone woman," who lay silent and safe in the village churchyard.

He was not a demonstrative man; but he had always felt a peculiar devotion for his one relation. Now that Polly had jilted him, the "lone" woman's memory was something to fall back upon, and he recalled numberless traits of tenderness, little things he had almost forgotten until that evening.

At last he came to a shed, surrounded by a low iron railing. It was full of carts. In one of these he could see straw beneath the seat. He got over the railing, and climbed up into it. Lying there, he thought of that lone woman who was six feet beneath the sod, his one relation. "To-morrow," he said to himself, "I'll sell my watch, and I'll go back home again."

Human nature *must* have a fetish.

If a man does not worship his own shadow, he falls down before the shadow of some one else. When these things fail to satisfy, he calls out for God Almighty, be it Humanity, Zeus, or Justice.

CHAPTER XIX.

A LONG WALK.

THREE days later he stood outside London, in a country place, where he could see green fields and hear the rooks cawing in the trees. The trees had naked branches. Everything looked as it had done a year before, when he set out for London; only then it had been early spring, and now it was drawing near Christmas.

He had loitered on the way, sleeping in padding cans, and drinking in public-houses. He had only one shilling left. But he did not hurry; there was no reason for hurrying. He looked weak and ill. Sometimes he drew in his breath, and then a spasm of pain set him coughing.

He walked on a little way, but stopped to pull a piece of wood from a hedge for a walking-stick. Mud was half an inch thick on his boots.

Leaning against a stile, he looked vacantly into the distance. It was very quiet there. He could not see a human being or a dwelling-place; nothing but fields, trees, hedges, and the grey sky that seemed to shut the earth in with a heavy curtain.

Presently a boy came in sight, whistling, while he cut bread-and-cheese with a pocket-knife. A dog was with him. When the dog saw Jos it gave a growl, and run up to smell a tramp; it turned away with a sniff, and went on with its tail upright.

Jos asked the boy, " What time is it ? "

" Don't know," was the answer. " It was twelve when I left home; and I've been on the road an hour most likely."

"" Can I get through the park ? "

" It's shut to tramps and vagrants."

Jos did not know his way exactly. He had been to villages near home and to market towns, but never to this place. Elmsworth lay six miles from a railway station, and the people there were just as primitive as in a Yorkshire village. The women seldom went to market, for the native shop supplied all their necessities, and a carrier called once a week with meat.

The men sometimes went to a neighbouring town ; one or two had been to London.

Jos could remember an old carter who had been taken to Paddington by mistake. This man had said to him, " I'd a mind to see what it was like on the railway, just to go one station on and back again. But no one told me to shift till I found myself in Lunnon. Then the guard, he shifted me. It wasn't likely I'd shift without being told ; now, was it ? "

Elmsworth stood on a hill, surrounded by thick woods. The squire was an old man of conservative habits. He let his game enjoy life. He would not even allow the farmers to shoot rabbits. Partridges ran across his garden, and nothing frightened hares but a big bell that rang morning and evening to tell the labourers when it was time to begin and when it was time to leave off working. His cottages held five hundred people, who had intermarried so much that almost every one was somebody else's relation. Two or three small farmers rented land from the squire ; but farms did not pay, and cottages were empty. Near the church stood the rectory, a low, white-washed house covered with vines and creepers ; and

close by was a room used for village clubs and
school treats. The rector let the Methodists
hold services in this room on wet Sundays.
Indeed, he would have put the Methodist
parson into his own pulpit, if it had not been
for the bishop. There never lived in this
world a more genial and tender-hearted man
than John Datchett.

Jos found a park gate open, so he went in,
although a board said that no admission was
allowed to tramps and vagrants. The green
grass stretched further than he could see ;
withered bracken and dead leaves lay thick
on the earth beneath the trees. As he walked
along without thinking where he was going, he
heard the birds singing in the leafless branches.
Then he said to himself, " I wish I'd stayed
down here. I wish I'd never gone to London."

Hours passed by while he walked across the
park. He often, sat down to rest, and he
would have gone to sleep if it had not been
so cold and damp. At last he came out in a
village, almost opposite an inn called the
" Punch Bowl."

" I'll get a bed in a barn," he said, " and a
glass of spirits."

He turned into the public-house where he found the host standing behind the bar, gossiping with half a dozen customers. A wooden bench ran along the wall, and sitting down there, with a pewter mug on his knee, he listened to the conversation. Behind the bar, in a small parlour, were the *élite* of the village; in front stood, or sat, five or six carters and peasants.

"Well, I've had my say," remarked a young man in the parlour, holding out a long pipe and looking at it. "The country's going to the dogs along of these foreigners. I'd like to weed 'em out; but, to do that, we'd have to begin down here in Windsor."

"Who'd there be then to shoot the pheasants?" asked an old man with white hair, dressed like a gamekeeper. "Things aren't what they were. When I think of all the big nobs who used to come down here shooting in the Prince Consort's time, I says to myself as there's something wrong somewhere. Now, I took the last gun from him, so I ought to know, seems to me, though I haven't seen the world like you young fellows."

'Shoot the pheasants!" laughed the younger

man. " Shoot you, more likely! You know you've to keep a good look out when Prince Henry's shooting. These foreign chaps know nothing about sport ; they're dangerous."

" Well," said the old gamekeeper, " I'm not going to say as Prince Henry doesn't keep me all of a cold shiver when he's got a gun with him, but it mostly comes because I can't make out his gibberish. I'm sorry for him, I am. He's dull here in Windsor."

" I've heard say at the Castle as the Queen keeps him mighty strict," said the host.

" I'll not have a word said against the Queen," exclaimed the old gamekeeper. " Fifteen years back, when I was ill with rheumatics, she came to see me. It isn't every man can say as the Queen's been to see him. I was in bed, and that bad in my joints I couldn't move myself. She's getting up in years, and, if she can't do what she used to, I'm not the man to forget that she came to see me when I'd rheumatics."

" It's nothing to do with the Queen that the land doesn't pay, and farms is empty," remarked the host. " She's done her best with this Jubilee business."

The younger man burst out laughing.

"I've heard nothing better than that," he declared, "not this twelvemonth."

The old gamekeeper shook his head.

"You young folks always want to turn the world upside down," he said; "but thank God you can't do it. When you're as old as me, young man, you'll think different."

Jos heard no more than that, for he fell asleep with his head against a wall, and his legs under the wooden seat.

The host woke him up.

"Can I sleep in a barn, or somewhere?" he asked.

"Yes, I've a place at the back," answered the host; "there's plenty of straw in it."

The following morning he tramped on through the forest. He did not meet a man or a woman there the whole day; the leafless trees and the dull grey sky were all he had for company. He was not hungry or thirsty; he was only conscious of a general numbness. The wind howled round him, making his teeth chatter and his ragged clothes shake.

At last he stopped, and bent down to pick up something that lay at the foot of a tree. It was a little dead squirrel that had died there from cold or hunger. He felt its stiff body, and looked at its closed eyelids. Its head fell over his hand, and its limp hair made him shiver.

Then he remembered its namesake.

He had not thought about Polly while on tramp, except to mutter sometimes, "The little hypocrite!"

Nothing kills love like contempt.

It is easy to love some bad men, difficult not to love some bad women, but well-nigh impossible to care for a poverty-stricken character.

While tramping his mind had been fixed on his native place, the past had filled all his consciousness. His one wish had been to get away from the city, to get back home again.

But now he thought of the Squirrel, and said to himself that he had been very selfish. She could not have known what had taken place, or have guessed why he had tramped away into the country. And the little thing had been so good to him!

He laid the dead squirrel down under the

tree, and walked on ; but presently he stopped. Then he went back to make a grave for it. Had any one been there to see, he would have left it to be eaten by flies and insects ; but he was alone in the forest, and as he covered it up he thought of its namesake.

That night he slept under a hay-rick.

The next day he tramped on in the same fashion. But now the road was familiar; every stone and tree had a place in his memory. Here and there he noticed slight alterations— hedges that had been ditched, and sheds that had been thatched during his absence. More than once he hid behind a tree, for he could see men working in the fields, and women picking up sticks. He did not wish the villagers to know that he had come back home like this ; he, Joseph Coney, who a year before had gone away to the great city. What he meant to do in Elmsworth it is difficult to think. He went there because he was "out of work," penniless. Besides, he felt ill.

" Maybe," he said to himself, " I'm dying."

Late one evening he stood close to the village inn, the " Two Pheasants," from which place he could see smoke rising up out of the squire's chimneys, and the church tower in the distance.

Two little children, who were passing by, stopped to look at him. They ran away screaming. He remembered the words of the dock-labourer,

" If children see you coming they run away, and women treat you like Old Nick."

He laughed. Elmsworth had never before heard a laugh so full of bitterness.

The people should not see him, he said to himself. He would go to the churchyard. Then he would tramp on. Perhaps he would go back to London ; but not to-night. To-morrow. To-night he would sleep in some ditch, where no one could see his rags and his wretchedness.

So he crept along by the hedges to the wood, in which, years gone by, a tramp had been found dead, a tramp whose death had been handed on as a myth from father to son, because the verdict had been " death from starvation."

There he lay down in an empty saw-pit, where the wind had blown dead leaves up against tall chalk walls, leaves in which there

was some warmth and comfort. Lying there
he thought more than once of the little dead
squirrel. The touch of its limp hair had made
him shiver.

CHAPTER XX.

THE SQUIRREL.

AFTER watching Jos go into the gin-shop, the Squirrel turned slowly away, and went towards Charing Cross station. Her face was very white. She scarcely looked up from the pavement. When she reached Villiers Street, some flower-girls called out,—

"Well, Squirrel, what's become of 'im?"

She took no notice, but asked, "Where's my basket?"

"Look here," said one of the girls, "don't tease her. She's a good little thing. She lent me twopence last week. I'll give it you back again, you know I will, Squirrel. Here's your basket. Never mind what they say. They're jealous."

"Why, Squirrel," said another girl, "don't you remember the little Italian boy who couldn t talk any English? He took all your money didn't he? He went away, and left you nothing but his box, with a dead guinea-pig in it."

The other girls laughed, and, as the Squirrel walked off with her basket, she heard them singing,—

> "I wouldn't be a bobby,
>   Sometimes they catch it 'ot;
> I wouldn't be a bobby,
>   I wouldn't be En-da-cott."

(Just then policemen had a bad time of it.)

She stood all the afternoon by the post-office watching for Jos; but he did not come there. Hour after hour passed by. People came and went. At last she had an empty basket. Then she slowly walked towards the Embankment. The basket remained fastened round her neck, although no flowers were in it. She seemed scarcely conscious of her surroundings, and often she jostled against passers-by, who said,—

"Look out! Where are you going to?"

At last she reached the obelisk, and stood still, looking up at it. A policeman watched her, but he did not say "Pass on." Few people spoke harshly to the Squirrel. Her eyes remained fixed on the summit of the obelisk ; and she was dazzled by the light that surrounded it. She could neither read nor write ; but she knew the inscriptions on its pedestal. Jos had read them to her, the morning they woke up near it, after the night spent on a neighbouring bench. He had told her then that the obelisk must be very old indeed ; and had said,—

" A man in the Bible built it, a Pharaoh who lived 1,500 years before Christ."

" Who's Pharaoh ? " the Squirrel asked.

" A king who was drowned in the Red Sea,' said Joseph Coney.

" Who's Christ ? "

He told her the story of the Cross.

" Poor gentleman ! " said the Squirrel. " Do you really think they treated 'im as bad as that ? Well, it 'appened a long while back, so let's 'ope the story isn't true, Jos."

All the religion that ever came into her life the Squirrel learnt from that obelisk, and from the sphinxes that guard it. Upon the breasts of those sphinxes were mystic signs that even Jos could not interpret. The woman's face, with an unfathomable smile on its massive features, fascinated her. The strong muscular body of the beast, with paws stretched out, perplexed her. She had never seen any one half-woman, half-animal, not even in a penny-gaff; yet she felt that such a creature must exist somewhere, otherwise how could it lie there on the Embankment?

Those sphinxes, too strong to be petulant, who smiled at the enigma of life, instead of asking, "Why?" "Why?" through half a century, who seemed to say, "It is childish to rebel against the limits of conscious existence, if we cannot interpret the universe, we will smile at the mystery around us," had a powerful influence upon the Squirrel.

Once, years gone by, she had climbed up to one of them and kissed its foot, overcome by its strength and her own weakness. It looked down on her with an unfathomable smile. It was like the blue sky, into which she could look and look, and yet see nothing but the sun smiling.

She stood for some time silently gazing at the birds and the fishes carved on the surface of the obelisk. No one was there but the policeman, and by-and-by he walked away, leaving her alone with the sphinxes. She went down the steps through the iron bars to the river, and watched the little waves curling on the stones, breaking against the wall of the Embankment.

Big Ben chimed seven as she stood by the water ; then she said to herself, " Perhaps I'll find 'im at 'ome." She went quickly towards the East End, and did not stop until she reached the doss-house.

The " 'ungry " man was there eating some supper. A dozen women were cooking by the fireplace, and a dozen men were playing " Man and homan " at the long table.

"What's become of Jos ?" asked the deputy's wife. " I 'aven't seen 'im this long while."

" 'Asn't 'e been in all day ?" inquired the Squirrel, trembling.

" 'E's not been 'ere to-day nor yesterday. I've 'ad to let the slip at the top. I couldn't keep it for 'im. 'E'll 'ave to turn in with the others if 'e comes to-night. Why, Squirrel, what's up ? You look like a white cat. Is Jos ill, or anything ?"

" 'E got run in yesterday," the Squirrel said ; "I bailed 'im out, and 'e went into a public-'ouse."

" I guess 'e's 'ad a drop too much," remarked

17

the deputy's wife. " Maybe they've locked 'im up again."

The Squirrel was restless. She went to a cupboard, from which she brought out a black cat, and two small black kittens. These she carried to the fireside in her pinafore ; but she soon put them back in their old basket. The "'ungry" man looked at her from beneath his blurred eyelids ; even he could see that she was not happy. She refused to eat any supper, although more than one woman offered her soup with potatoes and bread in it. The Squirrel often gave the lodgers scraps, and lent them halfpence. In fact, the deputy used to say, " It's a good thing her skin won't take off and on, for if it did she'd be sure to lend it to some one."

At twelve o'clock the lodgers went to bed, the "'ungry" man lay down on the heap of rags that he received gratis, and the Squirrel crouched beside the wooden chair of the deputy. Her eyes were fixed on the entrance ; but Jos did not open the door. Men and women came in for a night's lodging, paid the fee, and went upstairs to turn in anywhere they could find a bed vacant. The Squirrel sat by the fire, watching the red coals, and listening to the snores of the deputy, until two o'clock; then she rose up, and fastened round her neck the flower-basket. It was a long walk from the doss-house to Covent Garden, and to arrive there after half-past three was useless. All the best flowers would be sold by that time. If she came there later she would have to pay double price for rubbish.

The city was very quiet. Sometimes she met a man hurrying home from a place of amusement, once or twice she passed a woman smoking a cigarette; but by the time she reached Covent Garden all idle people had gone to bed, only busy men and women were beginning work before daybreak.

The market was lighted by gas, so she could easily find her way to the flower-stall at which she always bought her flowers. She was accustomed to the deafening noises, the rumbling wheels, and the angry voices, that surround the place soon after midnight.

" I tell you, you did," she heard a man say to a woman.

" Very well then, I didn't."

" But you did ! "

" I didn't."

" For Christ's sake move away."

" I ain't going to move for nobody."

At the flower-stall sat a little girl no older than the Squirrel, who came to the market with her father at two o'clock, and stayed until eleven in the morning, selling flowers and plants. She was perched on a high stool, and her feet rested on an old market basket.

" I've kept you some lovely ones," she said to the Squirrel. " You needn't have more than you like, I can sell 'em later on; the fern's twopence. You'll bring me a cup of tea directly they open at Lockhart's, won't you?" she pleaded. " I can't leave the flowers, and daddy must mind the fruit. I get so cold by six o'clock."

" I'll not forget," said the Squirrel. " You look after my basket. I'm going to lie down somewhere. When I come back to tie the flowers up, I'll bring your breakfast."

Then she went to a place full of old orange-boxes, and crept in between the wooden cases. She had often slept there; but that morning sleep would not come to her,—she lay awake thinking of Jos, wondering what had become

of him. All round her was a busy hum of
voices, and on her face shone a jet of gas.
She was covered up with a mat, and her head
rested on a box. As the hours passed by she
clasped her hands so tightly together that the
nails ran into her flesh, and she said,—

"'E'll never, never come back again."

Who can explain psychological presentiments?
Scientific men treat them with silent contempt;
yet they are states of consciousness that ought
not to be scoffed at. In moments of intense
joy, or of great sorrow, men and women sometimes become seers and prophets. Past scenes
are illuminated for them by a lurid light that
interprets enigmas and reveals secrets; coming
events seem to say "Such will be our history."
When they repeat these things, people tell them
"You ought to be burnt as a witch," or, "You
would baffle all the Jesuits." Yet these things
are but higher states of consciousness, which
patiently await the psychological stethoscope!

At six o'clock she crept out from among
the orange-cases, and went to Lockhart's.
She carried a large mug full of tea, and some
bread-and-butter, to the little girl at the stall.
It was too early for work; so she sat down on

a step to fasten the ferns and flowers with wire, ready for her basket.

Presently she went to the public-house where Jos had gone in to have some gin the previous morning. She pushed open the doors, and asked the publican, "'As a young man been 'ere, what left Bow Street yesterday at twelve o'clock, with 'is eye bound up by a pocket-handkerchief?"

"Bless your pretty features," said the publican; "do you think I notice all the gaol-birds I get here? No, I don't remember any one of the sort. Is he your sweetheart?"

The Squirrel went silently away. She stood at the corner of the square selling flowers all morning. Her large eyes had black rims beneath them, and their pupils seemed to touch the iris. Her little cold hands trembled so much that she dropped the pence on the pavement, and had to pick them up again. She had eaten nothing all day; but she was not hungry.

It was five o'clock when the last flower had passed from her basket into the button hole of a man on his way home from business. Then she went to the doss-house.

" 'As Jos been 'ere ? " she asked eagerly.

The deputy shook his head, and said, " I can't think what's become of 'im."

She went to the London Docks and St. Kit's ; but the men at the gates told her that they had not seen Jos for weeks. It was the same tale in the public-houses. Where could he be ? How was it possible for him to live without any money ?

At last she remembered the pawn-shop. He had often said that he would fetch away his mother's watch, and sell it ; but seeing him hesitate, she had made it possible for him to keep his fetish. Now she seemed to know that he had sold the watch, for how else could he pay his way, by what other means was it possible for him to live without a penny ? She had been to the casual wards of the workhouses in the neighbourhood of the square, and the masters had thought that she was his sister.

" He ain't here, my dear," they said. " If he comes, I'll let him know that you're looking for him. His name is what ? "

" Joseph," said the Squirrel, " Joseph Coney."

It was getting late by the time she reached
the pawn-shop. A boy was putting up the
shutters outside, and inside an old woman was
clearing away the rubbish.

" A young man with a silver watch," the
old woman repeated after the Squirrel,—" a
young man named Joseph Coney ? Why,
yes, honey. He was here this morning. I
gave him seven shillings for it. He's gone
away, back to the country."

Every trace of colour left the Squirrel's
face. She trembled, and caught hold of the
counter.

" What is it, honey ? " asked the old woman,
peering into her face. " What's he done to
you ? You look like a corpse. Maybe he'll
come back again. What is it ? "

" Nothing," answered the Squirrel. Then
she left the shop. She ran quickly along the
streets to the Bank, and on, on, to the
Embankment. She scarcely stopped until
she reached the obelisk. There the sphinxes
looked down on her with unfathomable smiles
that seemed to say,—

" He's gone away, back to the country."

It was dark on the Embankment, but for

the dim gas lamps ; a thick mist covered the river, a fog veiled the sky. Sometimes a carriage or a cab dashed past with lamps like glow-worms on it. All else was wrapt in darkness.

The Squirrel went through the iron bars, and lay down on the steps by the river.

She was in the grip of loneliness. Besides, her heart beat so fast that the thuds hurt her. Her sun had set, and would never rise again. Jos had gone away, he had gone into the country. Her horizon was very limited. Born in a doss-house, and left there by her mother, she had "tumbled up" among strangers. People had been kind to her, for she had been generous ; and her great eyes had given her pathos. But no one had touched her heart except Jos, and the little Italian boy, who had run away, and left her nothing but his box with a dead guinea pig in it. What her feeling had been for Jos, it is impossible to say ; for to know that one must have felt equally lonely.

Hours passed by, and she lay still on the stone steps, with her head buried in her arms, and her body stretched towards the river. No one was there, for when the policeman passed by he forgot to turn his bull's-eye on the steps, he did not suspect that a "waif and stray" lay there, hopeless.

At last she moved close down to the river, so near that she could feel its icy touch, although she could not see it. Death meant peace ; death was the end of everything. If she were to die, this horrid pain must go away ; she would forget all about Joseph Coney. There was nothing to live for. The future would be like the past, all loneliness. Jos had gone away. He had left her very, very lonely.

The water then seemed to begin singing. For the wraith Suicide had floated silently down the river.

With her were the souls of unborn babies, whose mothers had been drowned in the Thames. They cooed in the Squirrel's ear.

"Not to be, is much better." Afterwards Suicide sang a weird song, set to strange music. It was about the young man whose ambition had been vanquished ; the girl whose flesh-and-blood god had proved a fetish ; the mother whose son had followed vain women ; the father whose daughter had sold her honour for nothing.

The Squirrel thought that the water was singing ; and she crept nearer and nearer to the little waves that broke on the steps, that splashed against the stone parapet.

But Suicide was there, waiting for her.

A new note rang out, called Despair ; and it said, " There is no beginning, and no end. All things are, because they must be.

"Worlds revolve round the sun. The sun and its planets move round sister systems. The universe, huge and imperishable, turns round, round and round. Eternal life! Eternal death ! All things the same, only in different shapes. Nothing immutable, everything changing place. To put off this mortal coil means cessation of consciousness."

The Squirrel thought that the water was singing. She sprang up, and went to look at the face of the sphinx. The lamp shone upon it. Its unfathomable smile had no comfort for her. She crept on to the stone pedestal, close to the parapet. Then Suicide sang the story that Jos had told her, set to the key of utter loneliness.

" The bitterest cry that earth has ever heard rings still in the universe. It will never die.

It is born again and again. It can have no ending.

"'My God! My God! Why hast Thou forsaken me?'"

"'It is finished!'"

With one cry of "Oh, Jos!" the Squirrel sprang into the river. There was a struggle, a vain attempt to clutch at the slimy wall of the Embankment, a muffled groan. Then Father Thames drew her into his strong embrace; and she was no longer "a waif and stray," no longer lonely.

CHAPTER XXI.

HIS MOTHER'S GRAVE.

JOS woke up the next morning in the saw-pit. He could not think at first where he was, for the wind blew the branches about above his head, and whirled the dead leaves against the chalk walls around him. It was a dull November day, without a ray of sunshine to enliven the heavy grey sky. He tried to stand up, but his stiff limbs gave way, and he fell back again on the heap of leaves beneath which he had been sleeping.

The church clock struck eight, and then the squire's bell rang for breakfast.

The stillness was not broken again for half an hour; but after that he heard wheels, and raising himself on his elbow, he saw a light trap going rapidly down the hill, through the trees. Two young men sat in it; and they sang—

"When my dear wife died,
    I laughed until I cried,"

as they jolted along to market.

He staggered to his feet, and went to the foot of the hill. From that spot he could see the village.

"When it's dark," he said to himself, "I'll pay the churchyard a visit; then I'll tramp on. Maybe I'll go back to London."

Afterwards he looked about for a tree on which he had years gone by cut his name, "Joseph Coney." He could not find it for a long time, but at last he discovered the letters deep in the bark of an old trunk. He had cut them there one Sunday morning, on his way home from church, and he had talked to his mother, while cutting them, of all he would do later on, after he was a man, and able to earn his own living.

The "lone" woman had little guessed then how it would one day be with him.

She had died of bronchitis five or six years before he went to London.

He thought of the day when the coffin had been carried down the old staircase. The neighbours had come in to commiserate with him, but their voices had sounded far off, and he had felt very desolate. He had stood in the church like one dreaming, and had shivered from head to foot when a handful of earth had fallen from the hand of the sexton, and the clergyman had read the words of the funeral service. He had stumbled over the graves, and had gone home again while the bell was tolling. The cottage had seemed so empty! While he was sitting alone in the kitchen, the door had been opened by John Datchett. He could not remember what the clergyman had said to him; but the words had been something like this: " If in the hair you kissed with all your tenderness had been that crawling, slimy thing Deceit; if in the eyes you trusted had nestled those cankerworms, Low Purpose and Worldliness; if the one you loved had been buried alive, Jos, instead of being dead and buried, what would you have done then?"

" I'd have turned away, laughing!"

"Yes," answered the clergyman, "unless you had felt that by making your life one long prayer, you might perhaps save her!"

Jos had not understood then what the clergyman meant; but now he knew John Datchett's secret.

He went back to the saw-pit, for the wood led to a neighbouring hamlet, and he did not wish the villagers to see him. He lay there among the leaves, half awake, half asleep, scarcely conscious. Once he looked up, for he heard the huntsman's horn close by, and he knew, if the hounds scented a tramp, they might worry him to death. They had once nearly killed an old woman who had been picking up sticks near the saw-pit. But they ran along, with their noses close to the ground; and presently he heard the huntsman's horn far away in the next valley. He was too weak to feel hungry; all he wanted was sleep. He lay there in a semi-conscious state, out of which nothing roused him, unless a spasm of pain set him coughing. The wind swept in gusts through his old coat and his ragged trousers to his flesh. He would have felt cold, had he not been so drowsy. Drink had given him a fictitious strength, which was fast ebbing away, now that he could not get any more spirits. But the craving for gin had died out within him. He was neither hungry nor thirsty. His head was heavy, and his limbs were stiff. Had a public-house been close by, he would not have gone to it.

The afternoon closed in, and still he lay in the saw-pit, half buried in dead leaves, with his face to the earth. Had the villagers discovered him lying there, like a dog or a stick, they would have found it difficult to believe that this could really be Joseph Coney, the young carpenter, who a year before had started for London in such good spirits.

At last it was seven o'clock, and as dark as midnight. Then he got up, and went towards the church. He kept close to the hedges all the way, and walked slowly. Sometimes he stopped to watch the lights in the village. Once he said aloud, "I'd like to have a look at the place where I used to work." But he was afraid to go near the houses. So he walked across a field that led to the church, and went into an adjoining thicket. Lights streamed through a window in the south aisle, and lit up the white tombstone above his mother's grave. Looking up he could see figures in the organ loft, men and women singing. Then he heard voices.

"Lead, kindly Light, amid the encircling gloom,
                Lead Thou me on."

The voices stopped, but they began again,

"Lead, kindly Light, amid the encircling gloom,
                Lead Thou me on ;
        The night is dark, and I am far from home,
                Lead Thou me on."

It was a choir practice.

He wondered where they had buried John Datchett! His mother lay under an old fir tree, .near the children's burying-place, little things, for some of whom he had made coffins. Each family had a spot to itself, railed in and planted with flowers ; but the children had their own burying-place, to which they were carried by their schoolfellows. He thought that he would like to see where they had laid the clergyman ; but he was afraid to leave the thicket. He thought that the singers might perhaps recognise him.

At last the music stopped, the lights were put out, and the choir went home to supper. When the gate was locked, and the footsteps had died away, he left the thicket. He groped his way to the tombstone that had " Silent and

Safe ' written upon it. There he lay down.
He stretched out first an arm, then a leg, as
the men do on the grass in the London parks,
the men who are " not wanted "; and he laid
his head on the mound of earth beneath which
lay his one relation. He could hear owls hoot-
ing in the thicket, and dogs barking in the
village; but it was much quieter there than in
London. The wind had gone down. He was
too tired and faint to feel cold or hungry. He
only knew that his mother lay there, and that
close by was John Datchett. He had guessed
the clergyman's secret.

Those words came back to him with a new
meaning, " If in the hair you kissed with all
your tenderness had been that slimy, crawling
thing Deceit; if in the eyes you trusted had
nestled those cankerworms, Low Purpose and
Worldliness; if the one you loved had been
buried alive, instead of being dead and buried,
what would you have done then?"

He did not laugh, for he was far away from
the great city; he only said to himself, " Poor
little hypocrite!"

Presently he seemed to hear music, a solemn
chant that ran along the ground, and echoed

all round him. He had never heard music like it, not even in St. Paul's Cathedral, where he had often sat when "out of work," among the sad rows of men who go there because they are "not wanted."

He fell asleep listening to the music.

When he woke it was midnight. He struggled to his feet. An icy hand was on his throat, and he was gasping for breath. He fell heavily against the tombstone, and then back on the grass. Sweat came on his forehead, and his body grew rigid. He seemed to see in a glance all his past life, to recall every word, deed, and thought, in an instant. Then the vision vanished. The cold sweat wrapt him round like a burial garment ; and the icy hand closed so tightly on his throat that the death rattle came into it.

He knew then that he was dying.

In that moment of his mortal agony, when alone with Death, a hoarse whisper was heard in the darkness,—

"Help me, O God, for I cannot help myself!"

When it had left his lips, a strange peace filled his consciousness.

He had passed beyond the creeds, and

above the churches, to the very foot of the Absolute.

As it died away in the night he fell asleep, with his mother and John Datchett.

CHAPTER XXII.

PEACE AT LAST.

THE next morning at eight o'clock the church bell tolled twenty strokes, and stopped. Presently it began again, one, two, three, four, five, six; so the villagers knew that the dead man or woman had been twenty-six years among us.

The new rector was feeding chickens in his granary plot, when the bell commenced tolling. He put down the basket to listen, and he did not see the chickens jumping upon it.

"Who can be dead?" he asked himself.

He went to the belfry, where the old sexton was eating breakfast, with one foot in the noose of the bell rope.

"Who is it?" he asked.

"It's a young man, sir, that went to London a year from this. His mother was a lone woman, and his father died of drink. He was found dead on his mother's grave this morning."

"Where is he?" asked the vicar.

"We've laid him on the altar, sir; and we've sent word to make him a coffin at the place where he used to work."

The rector went down the belfry steps, and into the church. He passed up the side aisle, and through the iron gate of the altar railings. He lifted the altar cloth.

There lay the dead man, smiling.

His hands were folded on his breast; his eyes were shut; on his lips was a smile from the Absolute.

"Poor fellow!" murmured the rector; then he added, " How happy the poor fellow looks."

Later on the dead man was placed in a wooden coffin, and carried to the " Two Pheasants" where they held an inquest. The doctor said that his death must have been brought about by starvation, for his body was nothing but skin and bone, he had scarcely any flesh. But the jury did not agree in their verdict, because a penny was found in his waistcoat pocket.

This was the money he had asked the Squirrel

to give him outside the gin shop the morning he left Bow Street.

The villagers came to see him laid in the grave of the lone woman, whose husband had died of drink. They spoke in whispers, for they had known him as a boy. They had seen him in church, and had heard him whistling over his work.

"Earth to earth, ashes to ashes, dust to dust," said the priest.

This was the end.

So he came home again.

THE END.